City of Ulysses

Teolinda Gersão

CITY OF ULYSSES

Translated from the Portuguese by Jethro Soutar
and Annie McDermott

DALKEY ARCHIVE PRESS

Originally published in Portuguese by Sextane Editoria as *A Cidade De Ulisses* in 2011.

Copyright © 2011 by Teolinda Gersão
Translation copyright © 2017 by Jethro Soutar and Annie McDermott
First Dalkey Archive edition, 2017.

Library of Congress Cataloging-in-Publication Data
Identifiers: ISBN 9781943150175
LC Record available at http://catalog.loc.gov

This translation recieved support from the Calouste Gulbenkian Foundation.

Funded by the General Directorate for Book and Librarires—
Direção-Geral do Livro, dos Arquivos e das Bibliotecas / Portugal.

www.dalkeyarchive.com
Victoria, TX / McLean, IL / Dublin

Dalkey Archive Press publications are, in part, made possible through the support of the University of Houston-Victoria and its programs in creative writing, publishing, and translation.

Printed on permanent/durable acid-free paper.

AUTHOR'S NOTE

This book, which deliberately engages with the visual arts, is the result of my lifelong interest in that field and the many conversations I've had with artist friends over the years (João Viera among them, whom I single out by way of homage for he is sadly no longer with us).

I must give particular thanks to José Barrias: many aspects of the exhibition cited in Chapter III—writing as seduction, Ulysses' raft, *Almost a Novel*, recreating incredibly blue water, the installation *Nostos*, the letter to my father (entitled *The Image of a Shadow*)—featured in the exhibition *José Barrias etc.* held at CAM a few years ago, and I have recycled them freely. The concept of the *Maritime Ode* being written over the façade of the house where Fernando Pessoa was born was also José Barrias' idea: in 1995, he transcribed the text onto the walls of the poet's bedroom on Rua Coelho da Rocha, in an installation entitled *Um quarto de página (Reading Quarters)*. I'm also indebted to him for his support throughout the adventure that was the writing of this book, and for being its first reader.

I would also like to register my gratitude to everyone who has, over the centuries and right up until the present day, loved, studied, researched and recorded Lisbon. There are so many writers and books that it would be impossible to list them all here. But for the many I've read, and the many others I could not, I wish to express my deepest admiration.

T.G.

City of Ulysses

CHAPTER I

1.
In Search of an Exhibition

THIS WAS, HE said, just a preliminary chat, to give me an overview of the project and see if I'd be interested in taking part. A formal invitation would follow if I was. But I had no intention of committing to anything, I'd think about it and let him know in a few days' time.

We were in the director's office at CAM, the Contemporary Art Museum. His secretary, who'd called the previous week to make the appointment, had just come in, bearing two cups of coffee on a tray; through the window, I could see the gardens of the Gulbenkian Foundation.

I already knew the director, from when CAM had exhibited my work some years before. He obliged me with a little flattery, telling me he'd been following my career for the past twenty years and was a great admirer of my work. Then after a few more obliging comments, he got to the point:

He was planning to invite various artists to present a series of individual exhibitions based on their personal visions of Portugal. Given my profile, they'd decided at a recent board meeting that they'd like the first exhibition to be mine.

And, assuming I agreed, of course, they thought I could take Lisbon as my theme. Or rather my impressions of certain aspects of Lisbon, he clarified, putting his coffee cup back down on the tray.

I was taken aback by his proposal, but I didn't want to interrupt, and let him say his piece.

Lisbon is of course an inexhaustible subject, he continued, so we'll be asking other artists to approach it in their exhibitions too.

The exhibitions would open here and have a decent run, then tour several other countries. At this stage, he said, rounding off, he simply wanted to know whether I'd be interested. We talked a while longer, but I didn't ask any questions or seek to prolong the conversation. I promised to think the matter over and give him an answer within a few days.

I went outside and strolled around among the trees. The Gulbenkian gardens are very green, with almost no flowers. I always find the green soothing, so too the lines of the gardens, all horizontals and verticals. Trees and water. Sky, a lake, paving stones skirted by bushes, and broad stretches of grass.

I sat down on a seat in the small open-air amphitheater. There were other people there too, some reading books or newspapers, others—couples—embracing, and children running around on the grass below, under their mothers' watchful gaze. A group in tracksuits was practicing martial arts. Above us, a plane made its way across the sky, leaving a white trail that took some time to disappear.

The idea of this series of exhibitions made some sense. But why take it on tour? It was true that for millions of perfectly well-informed people across the globe, Portugal barely existed: at most, it was a narrow strip of land tacked onto the side of Spain. And Lisbon was probably the least known of all European capital cities, indeed one of the least known capitals anywhere in the world.

But what exactly was the aim of the project? For the artists to put Portugal on the map?

Ironic, really, in a country where culture has always been so chronically undervalued.

It would be easy to say yes, I thought, leaving the gardens and heading for my car on Avenida António Augusto de Aguiar.

Choose a point-of-view, a personal vision of the city. Nothing could be simpler. And then, with my sharp, unforgiving and sometimes cruel gaze, turn what I saw into a work of art. After all, wasn't that what I always did? This time, however, I was going to refuse. The only thing I felt inspired to do was get the matter resolved as soon as possible.

(Dear Sir,
Although honored and grateful for your invitation, I regret to inform you that I'll be unable to participate in the project due to prior commitments.
Yours faithfully,
Paulo Vaz)

A dozen or so words to that effect and never think about it again.

Then Sara phoned.
"Yes, I've just left the gallery," I said. "I'll tell you about it later. I'm going to say no."

I got into my car and pulled out into the heavy traffic moving towards Graça.
It was when the car in front stopped sharply at an amber light and I narrowly avoided running into the back of it that I suddenly imagined you, Cecilia, having that morning's meeting instead of me. Many years ago.
"This project actually already exists," you'd have told the director of CAM without hesitation. "Paulo Vaz and I have been working on it for a while. Assuming he agrees, we'd be glad to accept your proposal. I'll talk to Paulo and let you know in a few days."
And the director of CAM would have smiled, charmed, feeling that things could hardly have turned out better: he'd proposed a vague idea and you'd given him a concrete project in response, which had not only been planned but also, by the sound of it, was practically ready.

You would've come home and told me all about it, filled with enthusiasm and doubtless in fits of laughter. If the conversation had ever taken place.

And you wouldn't have been the least bit surprised by this extraordinary coincidence, in which something we'd dreamed up almost randomly seemed to have taken shape elsewhere, as if by magic, and sought us out via this prestigious institution.

You always believed in the impossible, so none of it would've struck you as particularly strange. Suddenly we were being offered all the resources we needed, and it was simply a matter of getting to work and bringing that long-imagined project to fruition.

But neither of us had ever taken the idea of an exhibition about Lisbon seriously. It was just for our own amusement, a private game to challenge each other's imagination. Wherever we went in the city we'd look around as if it belonged to us, as if we were going to make it into something else.

We went around on foot or on the Vespa I'd bought second-hand. It made an awful racket when it got going and always needed a kick-start, and then you'd sit behind, clinging onto me, your hair blowing in the wind. The most perfect image of freedom, or feeling of freedom, I've ever had, was speeding along with you, your arms wrapped around my waist, your hair flying in the breeze.

After a while we began wearing helmets and your hair no longer streamed out behind us. We still flew, though, down the cobbled and tarmacked streets. Runaways, is perhaps the best word to describe us in those days.

That was how I drew you back then: one foot still outstretched, as if you'd just climbed up behind me and the Vespa was already on the move. We're both seen from behind, a little dust kicking up, and your head, resting against my body, is turned slightly inwards, leaving your face only partially visible as the streets disappear around us, or we stop seeing them, aware of nothing but the speed we reach in a matter of seconds. Off we go, sitting up straight on the flat, leaning in on the curves. You give yourself over to our game of balance, swaying your body just the right amount.

That's what most of the drawings were of: movement and the play of opposites; the tension between precision and excess.

It was the first time you appeared in my work. Albeit with only half a face, and with speed blurring your contours.

You would've accepted the invitation right away, as long as I agreed.

"That's why I'm turning it down," I told Sara later. "It was a joint project, mine and Cecília's. It wouldn't make sense to do it without her."

Of course, I could always do something else, something totally different, I thought a few days later.

But the only thing that really interested me was going back to the project we'd dreamed up together all those years ago. We'd had the good sense not to take it too seriously at the time, but now, through sheer stubbornness, not only would I take it seriously but I'd also bring it into being. A real exhibition, in the real world.

"This project actually already exists; I worked on it with Cecília Branco a while ago. If she agrees, I'd be glad to accept the invitation."

I obviously couldn't say that to the director of CAM, Cecília. But nor could I present the project as my own.

Having pictured you in my place agreeing to the proposal, it occurred to me that I might be able to take the job on after all, as long as you were included. "*City of Ulysses*. An exhibition by Paulo Vaz, based on a project by Cecília Branco."

That way I wouldn't be stealing your ideas and passing them off as my own. I'd even credit you with the concept, though that wasn't entirely accurate. But it'd make up for the fact that the work was ultimately appearing under my name. And it would be a chance to recover all those things we'd thought up that would otherwise be lost. A new version of "Lisbon Revisited," with both our signatures.

It seemed like a simple solution, although nothing is actually ever simple. And nothing is ever as it seems, as experience teaches us time and time again.

Dear Sir,

I accept the invitation etc. in the hope that these touring exhibitions might be of some value to the country in these times of economic crisis, the very bowels of the crisis no less, a crisis that seems set to go on and on. And because this is, after all, my job: to exhibit my art.

That said, I am accepting primarily for personal reasons:

This is the second time I find myself considering an exhibition about Lisbon. As a rule, opportunities don't come around twice; we're usually lucky to be granted even one. Which is why I was initially so surprised and disconcerted by your proposal, and why my immediate reaction was to reject it as if it were a kind of trap.

And I remain convinced that it is a trap. Any exhibition about Lisbon, even one limited to certain aspects of it, is a minefield: thirty centuries of history are enough to addle anyone's perspective. Whatever the artist comes up with, it will never be more than a rough sketch, a work in progress, or whatever you want to call it. So I hereby declare my reservations, signed and on record. However, since you know all this as well as I do, I can only presume that a sort of work in progress is precisely what you're expecting. And if an institution as prestigious as your own is bold enough to embark on such a venture, I see no reason not to embark on it with you.

To be perfectly honest, I thought the idea foolish and not worth taking seriously when we first thought it up, myself and the woman I lived with at the time; a woman who was, incidentally, the most creative and gifted person I've ever known. For reasons I need not go into here, she can't be involved in the project now, and the collaborative relationship that once existed can't be revived. Nevertheless, and I'll gladly explain why in due course, her name should still be credited because it will still be a joint project.

Moreover, this is essentially why I'm accepting the invitation: the chance to return to a project that included her.

As I said, my reasons for accepting your invitation are very personal.

Most art emerges this way, as you're no doubt aware: for personal reasons, typically selfish ones; the pleasure artists derive from exerting control over reality and shaping it to their will.

And so I smile to myself as I write this, and I imagine you smiling too. A person goes to an exhibition and looks at apparently objective things. But their creators are always present inside them, present in life, body and soul, in everything—albeit also in camouflage. To exhibit is also to hide. And artists are masters of disguise, as you'll know only too well.

I won't, therefore, be exhibiting anything of myself. Artists exhibit their work, but never themselves. It's always pretend.

Which is why I'll of course never send you this letter, dear director. I'll merely send you, in the next few days, the standard two or three lines, conventional and as expected. I'll say that I gratefully accept the invitation. Everything else I'll naturally set to one side, out of reach of you and everyone else. After all, it's no one's business but my own.

Best wishes.

PS (I realized this was missing a postscript): Accepting the offer will mean distancing myself from another woman, a woman called Sara who means a great deal to me. It will be a mental distancing, but I won't say "only" mental. For better or worse, everything important in life also happens on an imaginative level.

At least, that's the way it is with artists. "La pittura è cosa mentale,"
Leonardo said in a different context, but it can be applied here too.
Much of my work has been inspired by passions of some sort;
women have always been a source of energy or a point of departure
for everything I've produced.
     And so it shall be this time. Memory, one should never forget, is
the mother of all muses.

But enough entertaining myself with witty little games and
imaginary Impossible Letters to the Director of CAM; enough
of the Gulbenkian, CAM, the director, the general public, critics
and whoever else. Time to set up my trestle and get to work.

Forgive me, Sara, for leaving you in the background for perhaps
a little too long. I'll tell you I've accepted the invitation, obviously, but I'll also do my best to keep you from feeling a distance
has come between us. Because from now on I'll be thinking of
another woman who's now back in the game, my game, our
game, and I know she's ready to play. We'll start at the beginning, which is where games should always begin.

The first time I saw you, Cecília, was in a classroom. Back then
I was a sort of assistant lecturer in one of the first-year courses.
But I never felt like your teacher; authority never suited me and
I didn't want to be a teacher anyway, I wanted to be an artist
full-time. Giving classes was a lesser occupation, a temporary
means of paying the bills, and I planned to give it up as soon as
I could. But you didn't know that then; we knew nothing about
each other and yet there we were, you and I, playing teacher and
student for a while.
     So I was able to observe you three times a week, sitting at
your desk, making notes on whatever I was saying (in one of
those tiny notebooks of yours). Or not writing anything down,
just staring back at me as if you were the teacher and I was being

examined. Would I pass your test? I asked myself as I returned to my own desk, behind which I felt more secure, and where I was able to consult my notes. But it wasn't my knowledge that felt exposed: it was my very being. You could see (examine, assess) the color of my eyes, the shape of my nose, my ears, my glasses, my hands, the clothes I was wearing, and, if I ventured close enough to the front row, where you sat, you could even smell the aftershave I'd put on that morning. You could accept or reject me. In the meantime, though, I stayed safely behind my desk, where you couldn't smell me and where, thanks to my glasses, it was harder for you to make out the color of my eyes.

I'd put my right hand in my trouser pocket and rest the other on my notes, for I'd noticed myself speaking with my hands and you, perhaps involuntarily, following my every gesture. My hands were distracting you from me.

A few minutes later I'd be back on my feet, springing out from behind my desk to pace around the podium. I was on a stage, putting on a show for an audience of one: you. I hoped you were interested in what I was saying, but even more than that, I hoped you were interested in me, the man who was saying it.

You weren't the only one observing me, but in the midst of all the other students, I'd always hone in on you, even while pretending to address the entire room. For a whole hour and a half I could take you in, all at once or gradually, savoring each detail: your light brown hair with a hint of blond, contrasting with your tanned skin, your big eyes, a cross between gray and green—or so they seemed, though I'd need to verify that, from closer up and in a different light. When, for example, I kissed you. Only then would I see exactly what color they were, in that second before you closed them and gave yourself over to the warmth of my mouth on your mouth, which by then would be smiling.

I'll never forget the sex we had, Cecília, though it wasn't the only reason I loved you.

You love a person just because you do; it's impossible to explain. Sex can't truly be spoken of, let alone described. The great mistake with pornography is the belief that sex can be made visible. It can't: it is done, felt, experienced; it is present in the skin, the body, the soul, the memory, but not in what the eye can see. Sex is invisible. Describing it is like describing a sea voyage without leaving the shore, analyzing the movement of the water and the ship's position without ever going aboard. When nothing but the journey is real. Only afterwards can it be spoken of, and even then only in a vague, approximate way.

It's true that I began by admiring your face and desiring your body. I noticed how you dressed, never ostentatiously or provocatively, but rather subtly and with an easy sophistication. Still, the way you dressed made me want to undress you.

What did I see in you that I didn't see in other women? What made you stand out within the confines of the classroom?

Beyond the initial, purely physical attraction and my subsequent longing to please you, it was your mental and emotional side that made me see you differently. I discovered you were sensual and brilliant and I gave in to the temptation of talking to you. Words played a decisive role in what happened between us. I realized that what I was looking for, on every level, was someone I could talk to. And that, in the end, was what I found. I'd thought I knew women, but I saw that with you I'd washed up on an entirely new continent.

Those long conversations in which we talked about anything and everything, going wherever the wind took us. We were carnal lovers, but intellectual lovers too, I came to realize. Something improbable was happening between us, something I'd always assumed didn't exist.

Making love to you and talking to you had much in common: with both, we'd abandon ourselves entirely to a kind of inner music, exciting one another, lost in our game of mounting tension, playing for pleasure alone. And then suddenly, when our bodies or words met, something exploded, shone bright, illuminated everything: love, or a particular vision of the world. We swapped experiences, discoveries, and memories, exchanged opinions that coincided or clashed. These things passed back and forth between us, and as they did so we were transformed. There was a before and an after meeting you.

And then one day you said, as if stating something self-evident: meeting you is the most important thing that's ever happened to me.

I discussed ideas with you that had interested me for a long time. Portugal, having only recently emerged from a dictatorship, was decades behind the rest of the world. In 1976, I'd received a grant to study in Berlin for two years. I ended up staying until 1980 and then hitchhiking around Europe, and throughout that time I came across many things that changed the way I thought. I became preoccupied by questions that probably had no answers, and perhaps didn't need them, because the questions themselves were stimulating enough.

For example, could modern art ever work as an entirely visual medium, without needing to be backed up by words? Or had it become nothing more than a pretext for fascinating exercises in hermeneutics, which arguably now occupied part of its space?

It was easy to say that a true work of art didn't need words; that words would always be redundant. The essence of the artwork could never be verbalized precisely because it belonged to another field entirely: the visual. Hence the name, the visual arts.

However, that wasn't entirely true. One school of thought

argued that the value of a work of visual art lay not in the piece itself but in the reactions it provoked, which could only be expressed in words. Curiously enough, what was said or written in response to a work of art sometimes turned out to be the most interesting thing about it. In a way, then, works of art were becoming a vehicle for something else, something above and beyond themselves. Were they vampires, secretly feeding on the blood of words? What if they were? That could be stimulating in itself, a new point of departure. Similarly, literature—the art of the written word—was spreading into and encroaching upon other domains, seeking new ways of becoming visible, as if the closed and silent world of books was no longer enough. We'd reached a turning point, in which art forms were contaminating one another and anything was possible: new ways of telling, showing, revealing, sharing, experiencing, visualizing. The reader-spectator-visitor had an ever-greater role. They could now enter works of art, move around inside them, losing and finding their way as they went.

As a creator, I liked to adopt an autocratic approach: to take viewers inside a world of my own making, one in which I set the rules. They could keep their distance if they wanted, and they were free to exercise critical judgment, but first they had to enter my work (or the broader space of the exhibition), and once inside they'd be trapped like a bird in a cage until they found their way out again. And while they were there, they'd be subjected to an experience, or a happening, which I got to control, to greater or lesser degrees. They agreed to look at whatever I put before them, and in a sense to see it through my eyes. Only afterwards were they free to see it again with their own eyes and reject any part of it they wished. That was their turn; the second stage of the game. But I always went first.

Creating was, by its very nature, an exercise in power; about this I was adamant. I wanted to control my viewers. Fascinate them, subjugate them, convince them; shock, annoy, provoke and delight them—to create emotions and stir reactions. And yes, it was a form of making love. For some reason, an artist's overall output, when the time comes to survey it, to navigate and decipher it, is known as a "corpus": a body of work. A piece of art is realized through an encounter, body to body. Two people, two perspectives, two visions. They might converge, in which case there is fusion, a relationship of identification and surrender, an almost physical pleasure; or they might diverge, in which case there is friction, intellectual argument or confrontation, and the pleasure is indistinguishable from the fight, the effort to convince—for convincing the other is a form of victory.

Such questions fascinated you too. The world around us was being transformed; anything was possible. Every era reinvents the world in a new way, but ours had new tools with which to do it, new technologies and new ways of using them. The perspectives were endless, the sky was the limit.

I remember we used to talk about installation as an art form: a hybrid, vampiric form that worked freely with disparate elements and invited visitors to cross three-dimensional thresholds. It was something that happened to the viewer, appealing to all the senses—sight, smell, touch, intellect—as if transporting them to another plane, another place, another life. An experience that, if taken to the extreme, might (or should) leave the viewer somehow changed. Because art—at least the sort that interested us—was neither harmless nor innocent. It was dangerous; there was always risk.

Throughout all this, I studied you in detail: your movements, your dress, your notebooks, your pen (never just any old biro), your sunglasses case, the ribbon or clip you wore in your hair— though I always preferred your hair hanging loose, falling over your shoulders, tickling the soft fabric of your blouse.

And at the same time I felt myself being studied by a very

young woman seeking a man to love. Nausicaa (it suddenly occurred to me) leaving home one morning, singing to herself, and finding a man washed up on the beach. Falling in love immediately, without knowing anything about him. Just because it was a beautiful morning and she wanted love, yearned for it with every fiber of her young body. She finds a man lying in the sand, plastered in salt; her servants flee, but she approaches him, unafraid. She's ready for their encounter; her whole life has been leading up to it, all previous mornings have converged upon this one. Which is why she dreamed of him the night before and left the house singing, and why she now sings all the way home.

I'll wait for you at my parents' house.

She knows nothing about the stranger, she doesn't know he's on a journey, that he'll be forever on a journey. She doesn't know he has another woman.

That won't come until the second moment, when he speaks. But until he speaks, her desire rules the world. If he doesn't tell his story, the first moment prevails, the moment she found him lying there asleep on the beach. And she loves him immediately because she's been waiting for him, because she's been waiting for love.

This image reminds me of the first time you came to my house, when I undressed you and lay you down on the bed. Later on, after we'd drifted off, exhausted, there came a point when I woke and saw you were watching me, that you'd perhaps been watching me for some time, naked and asleep, carried to wakefulness on the waves of sleep. As if we were on a beach and the sheets were an extension of the sand.

Naked and shipwrecked, I thought later. I'd already lived through various love stories, leaving broken bits and pieces in my wake. There was a part of me that was never quite satisfied, that led me to wander and drift. It was how I was and I couldn't change it. But I didn't tell you, and you didn't know.

I knew almost nothing about you either; only that we'd fallen in love the moment we met, because what else could we do?

It was around then I painted the *Nausicaa's Morning* series, caring little about context, interested merely in the moment: a shipwrecked man washed up on the beach, who regains consciousness and opens his eyes to see a very young woman looking down at him. It's a glorious summer's day and she brings him back to life: she gives him some food and some cloth and points him towards her home. She goes on ahead to prepare everything, to wait for him. She goes on ahead, singing all the way home. (I'm convinced she sang, even though it's not written anywhere that she did.)

Everything was the same that morning, when you woke up and went over to the window. But everything was different. It was the same street out there, the same houses, the same greengrocers, the same newsstands, the same people doing their daily shopping, exchanging the same pleasantries—"thank you" and "good day"—with the same people across the counters.

And yet it was all different, as if everything had changed and nobody had noticed but you.

Yes, the number 28 tram still passed, rattling the rails, used by locals in a few neighborhoods, but mostly by tourists for fun, as if it could transport them centuries into the past. And now another tram, a red one, which did a circuit of the Lisbon hills, coming up behind the 28, jangling along, adorned with little flags. And the post office at Praça de Camões was still there, with its windows and doors painted red, just like all the other post offices, and bearing the same logo, a postilion rider on horseback blowing his bugle. And the minibuses still took children to school; the cars still clogged up the road, stopping and starting; taxis still passed, typically full at that hour of the day, blocking the traffic while the driver unhurriedly wrote a receipt or counted out some change.

And when you reached Restauradores square, looked up towards Avenida da Liberdade and strode on, up its wide sidewalks, the trees were a soft green, new leaves appearing even though winter hadn't yet passed. Road sweepers tidied and plucked weeds from flowerbeds, stuffing them inside black plastic bags big enough to hide dead bodies in. Old folk sat on benches among the trees.

You passed the shops on either side of the avenue, and didn't need to look at the lettering in their windows to know they were advertising their latest collections. And there were the usual hotels, the Tivoli and the theater of the same name, the São Jorge cinema, café terraces yet to put their parasols up.

But everything, despite being the same as always, was completely different. Which is why you smiled to yourself, walking up the road in that strange state of grace, as if nothing bad could touch you, as if happiness were something real and palpable that you held in your hand, and would be yours forever.

You'd fallen in love as if entering another dimension. You felt powerful and life seemed easy, as if you'd never again experience difficulties or encounter obstacles in your path.

I listened to you, surprised. I'd unleashed this force in you without possessing it myself. I wished I had your gift for loving this way. Even knowing it was all an illusion. That the object of your love was incidental; a vibration, a mere spark that had lit your fire. You could've fallen for any man and he'd have made you feel the same, for this was how you loved. It just happened to be me. That was all. Deep down, I was irrelevant, though you thought quite the opposite.

But you went on talking, for days, weeks, months. Or so it seemed. As if nothing could break the spell or stem the flow of your speech. The city was lit up and everything you looked at seemed to relate to me: the yellow lettering on the *Pensão Josefina*, cheap guest houses advertising rooms with hot water, surreptitious signs announcing *Zimmer, Chambres, Rooms,* awaiting furtive lovers who'd disappear through doors, up stairs, into lifts, behind curtains.

You shone as if there was a light inside you. Had your voice been as strong as your desire, it would've thrown love to the four winds, sung it from the rooftops, shouted it from the mountains, printed it in the newspaper headlines. If I were to disappear, I thought with a start, your world would collapse. I was your ears' inner music, the air you breathed. You talked about me because you were full of me. You were pregnant with me, I realized with some concern. If you went on loving me this way, I'd be born. And I'd be as big as the world, because that was the extent of your love for me.

It frightened me to listen to you, and so I said:

Don't expect too much from me, Cecília. I'm a free-spirit, or unreliable, if you prefer. I'm just passing through. I'm older than you and I've learned from experience: love doesn't last.

Love doesn't last. One day we wake up and the charm has gone. The world is back to how it used to be. Back to nothing. That's what we have in store, Cecília. Love is a fiction that lets us hide from the void for a while, the void inside and outside all of us. You've never experienced that void, but one day you will.

And I worry you'll experience it through me, a cynical man, given to passions and sensual pleasures but incapable of love. Too selfish for love.

Love wears itself out over time and drives passion away. Or passion drives love away. It uses itself up and then seeks something else to use instead. That's what I'll do to you, more or less, even if I don't mean to. Which is why I'm giving you this warning: don't love me like this, Cecília. Love me with your body, and nothing more.

But when I said such things (and I know I repeated them over and over, ad nauseam), you had a particular way of not listening, of dismissing what I said as nothing but words.

You were so perfectly made for love. So conscious of being desirable and so pleased about it. Your body was tender and ripe as a fruit.

I remember floral dresses were the fashion then. There were flowers everywhere, in shop windows, on models in magazines and women in the street. It was as if you'd contaminated the world around you. The flowers on your dress blossomed everywhere and filled everything; your joy touched everything like sunlight.

Your amazing, indestructible joy. You didn't realize it, but you were subverting the world around you, ridding it of anything you thought wrong or useless.

Sometimes I'd study you curiously, as if you were an outside element, a case apart. You had a peculiar way of laughing and dancing, for example, of marking the time with your feet on the floor and clapping your hands in a rhythm that came from deep inside you, from the center of your spine. And then you'd start to dance, swaying your hips like an African woman. Love, you thought, was simple and joyous.

One afternoon at Guincho you wrote in the wet sand:

I, Cecília Branco, hereby declare an end to sadness. And to melancholy.

I smiled at your self-assurance, your visceral rejection of anything you thought dead or dated.

But things weren't really like that, I'd tell you. There was another side of the coin.

The other side. Melancholy, spleen, the sharp edge of the knife, the slanted rain that forever falls on this sun-kissed country.

Fernando Pessoa, with his quiet disquiet, who ended up alone at a café table getting drunk on a bottle of brandy, writing those ridiculous letters to an Ofelia who'd probably never read Shakespeare, who was happy just being Ofelia and certainly didn't feel inclined to drown herself in the Tagus when she realized the man who said he lived and breathed for her would never get beyond the breathing stage.

He lived and breathed for her, but only in theory, you said. (And as you'd say then: we ought to add some brackets here and take a deep breath ourselves.)

His coffee cup, his cigarette, his glass of brandy, the monotony of his days, the melancholy of the streets he walked in Baixa, his fondness for his mother's apron strings, his nostalgia for a time when he still celebrated his birthday and nobody he loved had died. That's right. Spleen, neurosis, melancholy. To be or not to be, or at least a tame, riverside version of it. Pessoa was practically nothing in life, but his trunk full of dreams—of unfinished, unpublished papers—helps us fill the void, or make up for our own lack of dreams. We share his addiction to getting drunk on what might have been but never was, what never took shape or moved beyond an initial sketch, what is forever unfinished—for then it might have become anything, anything in the whole world. Pessoa's is a bottomless trunk because our melancholy leads us inside it and we never find our way out. Mortal poetry, the sharp edge of the knife twisting in our flesh. The wound that won't heal. The word.

Searching for the right word. He scribbles away at the café table, in a cloud of smoke. And he chooses to live with neither man nor woman, does not choose a woman because perhaps he dreams of a man—listen, Daisy, when I die, tell that young lad he gave me many happy hours—but they were imaginary, those happy hours. He sits at a café table and drinks another glass of brandy, accepts his non-life, slips into the fantasy world of astrology, the fifth empire, mysticism, art, and black magic,

loses himself amidst the throngs in the street, as much of a
nobody as everyone else, gray figures all, in their overcoats, hats,
glasses, and jackets, weary of the winter cold, crossing the street
but never reaching the other side, each one with a foot raised
as if about to take a step, any step, provided it's a decisive one
and takes them somewhere, but in the photo they're frozen in
the act of crossing the street, with the wind—a gentle breeze,
nothing alarming—lifting the hems of their overcoats just
below the knee.

A muffled hysteria, which no one could see or hear. He
had only one book published in his lifetime, which practically
nobody read; his poems in magazines, his *Maritime Ode*, his
cries, his screams, his excesses, his warnings, all ignored. He
plunged himself into silence and alcohol, though he was also
a conscientious employee for a while, humble and obliging,
working nine to five in an office. At home, the housekeeper,
Senhora Adelaide, would leave a note: 'Senhor Pessoa, I had to
go out, your dinner is ready . . .'

You wanted to have your photo taken, like thousands of others,
sitting in the bronze chair beside the Pessoa statue outside Café
Brasileira. After that you forgot all about Pessoa, believing that
excessive attachment to him was a typically Portuguese disease.
One should get to know him, go through a Pessoa phase, and
then move on. Export him to other languages and continents,
deliver him promptly to readers everywhere, that was what the
information age was for. Use Pessoa to avenge the centuries
Camões had to wait before being read (and even then he was
never read enough); to avenge all the other Portuguese authors
who, for want of a translation, never made it beyond our borders.

An intelligent seat, you said, sitting down beside him.
Extremely intelligent. Every tourist wants to be photographed
there. No doubt they've never read a word he wrote, but he's a
good symbol of Lisbon. His only competition is São Vicente's

ship and crows on the city's coat of arms, although there aren't many crows in Lisbon anymore.

You could be pragmatic too sometimes. Or, as you put it, realistic and practical.

Yet you never quite managed to be realistic. Love, while it lasted, transformed everything.

And we were nothing like tourists. We were travelers, which is a different thing entirely.

Tourists go to new places as a way of escaping from themselves, from routine, stress, unhappiness, boredom, old age, death. They glance at the places they visit but never fully get to know them and quickly swap them for other places, trying to escape ever further away. Travelers, however, go in search of themselves in new places. And they get to know these places deeply: their desire to discover themselves is such that no effort is too great and no step too far.

Travel agents and tourists only care about real cities, of course. Travelers prefer imaginary ones. And with a bit of luck, they find them. At least once in their lives.

And, for once in our lives, luck was on our side. We found the city we were looking for. The City of Ulysses.

2.
In Search of Lisbon

A city we built for ourselves, unrestricted by the one already there. Because not even that one was real: of the ten million Portuguese citizens and two million tourists who walked the city's streets, each had their own image of Lisbon, the Lisbon they knew or that suited them best. And so we could touch the city without being afraid; we could (re)invent it at will.

We didn't spend all our time thinking about the city, of course. Most of the time we were thinking about ourselves. We followed our daily routine, like everyone else, and gathered impressions and sensations without even noticing.

(The sound of water lapping at the harbor wall, the smell of the sea drifting through the city on mornings of low tide, the sound of the street outside our house in Graça, which had no double glazing;

footsteps on the black and white cobbles, basalt and limestone patterns in the paving, the knife sharpener's whistle catching us by surprise, half-a-dozen happy notes in quick succession, sliding up a climbing scale, a mechanical holler all the more noteworthy for being, with the exception of the occasional lottery seller, the last cry of its kind, a sign of the times;

ashlars on walls that were hot to the touch on sunny summer days;

the wind rippling the surface of the river, sprinkling it with foam, the changing color of the water as the year rolled on by;

gangs of starlings on late winter afternoons, whenever we walked through Terreiro do Paço square or past the Cais do Sodré and Santa Apolónia stations, eating roasted chestnuts

from the street vendor, stopping to watch the birds in their
synchronized flight for a few minutes, their incredible speed,
their constant, rapid changes of direction–)

We'd notice things and then forget them a moment later.
We lived life in a hurry, like everyone else.

Lisbon was simply a backdrop, and generally out of focus
because our attention was on other things. Only every so often
did we look directly at the city.

If I'm now imagining a time in which we went in search of
Lisbon, it is only as a tool to help me with my work, to provide
some kind of structure and method. But I know such a time
never existed, I'm inventing it now, gathering up the fragments
to form something solid in my memory.

City of Ulysses. We found the name irresistible. The legend of
Ulysses founding Lisbon first surfaced over two thousand years
ago and there could be no ignoring it, no pretending it didn't
exist.

After all, Ulysses' journey had now been part of the European
imagination for almost three millennia. Hellenic civilization
was the cradle of Europe, and *The Odyssey* (much more than
The Iliad) had, for hundreds of years, been western civilization's
second great book, alongside the Judeo-Christian Bible. Just as
there was an approved 'vulgate' text of the Bible, so too was
there a Homeric vulgate, and beyond the vulgate, a fair few
stories did the rounds making use of the same characters.

Legend had it that Ulysses gave Lisbon his name, Ulysseum,
which then became Olisipo through an unlikely etymological
process.

This gave Lisbon a singular status: a real city founded by
a fictional character, a city contaminated by literature and
storytelling.

Joyce started from nowhere when he wrote *Ulysses*; Dublin
was a long way off Homer's character's imaginary course.

Lisbon, on the other hand, was historically linked to Greece by the maritime trading routes of the Greeks. (Even today, there are numerous Greek remains and ceramic fragments at Almaraz, near Lisbon, and elsewhere in Portugal, in places like Aveiro, Alcácer do Sal and the Algarve.)

So there was no need for us to invent a relationship between Ulysses and Lisbon. It'd been invented over two thousand years before, and because the story had legs it was still standing all these centuries later.

What traces of the myth could be found in Lisbon today?

A fair few, in fact: Ulysses Tower in St. George's Castle, which used to be the Torre de Tombo, where Fernão Lopes and Damião de Góis once wrote; a glove shop on Rua do Carmo called Luvaria Ulisses, sophisticated and as tiny as a tissue box; the Olisipo bookshop in Largo da Misericórdia; Ulisseia Filmes and Ulisseia the publisher. Fernando Pessoa even founded a press called Ulissipo, which printed his first collection of poems in English, as well as *Canções* by António Botto and *Sodoma Revisitada* by Raul Leal, before going bust. That was about it for mementos, at least in terms of those still visible today, but they formed a record of sorts.

By contrast, Gaius Julius Caesar had vanished from Lisbon completely, as if the great imperial divo hadn't in fact been here, in august person, in the first century of our age. As if he hadn't loved the city, hadn't been so happy here that he'd rechristened it in his own name, calling it Olisipo Felicitas Julia.

Lisbon may have forgotten Julius Caesar and the names Felicitas and Julia, but it'd never forgotten Ulysses. Who hadn't even set foot in the city, for the simple reason that he'd never existed. What's more, the power of his non-existence was such that it seemed to have contaminated his author: some said Homer had never existed either, that the story had been written by someone else, or indeed several others.

It was most likely the Phoenicians who founded Lisbon, at least half a millennium before Christ walked the earth, when they came to trade with the indigenous Iberian population. However, the Romans found myth more appealing than history: linking Lisbon to Ulysses allowed them to forget the Carthaginians (descendants of the Phoenicians in the north of Africa), who'd had the temerity to defeat the Romans in the Punic Wars and reach Lisbon before them. It also projected a sense of Greek cultural prestige onto a city that would have otherwise had the same municipal status as any other big city in the empire.

The Romans therefore had an interest in propagating the myth, and they used the various artifacts relating to the arrival of Hellenic civilization in this part of the world to do so. It was easy to link these remains to Ulysses and tell grand tales of a Greek Lisbon that came before Roman Lisbon, which itself began in 138 BC and left numerous ruins, including some that can still be visited today.

Ulysses' Lisbon was not, then, a Renaissance invention, though the myth was revived during that time when the ancient world provided both model and fashion. Neither was it an invention of our own. It wasn't our doing, for example, that Strabo wrote in his first-century *Geografia* that Lisbon had formerly been known as Ulisseum, having been founded by Ulysses, or that Solino and several others replicated Strabo's work. Nor did we prompt Asclepíades de Mirleia to describe a Minerva temple in Lisbon as being adorned with shields, garlands, and prow spurs in honor of Ulysses' wanderings, or Saint Isidore of Seville to declare, in the twelfth century, that "Olissipona was founded and named by Ulysses, in that place where the sky and the earth, the sea and the land divide."

It was only a myth, and as such a lie, but it would seem that not even saints tell the truth all of the time, and Isidore of Seville was no less a saint because of it. Nobody could be held to account when the writings came from such illustrious sources. These things always made us smile. For example, there was the day we took the ferry to Tróia, a small and narrow peninsula across the water from Setúbal, just a stone's throw from Lisbon. The place seemed determined to join in with the myth. There was its name for a start, of unknown origin—a name so inexplicable it could only have been Ulysses' doing, we joked, aware that others had made the connection before us. Tróia, named after Troy, the war-torn city from which Ulysses was returning home.

It was easy to imagine these things, lying on a near-deserted beach on a sunny, windless April day.

We traced Ulysses' route in the wet sand with a stick of driftwood: he'd sailed across the Mediterranean, threading through the Strait of Gibraltar (called the Pillars of Hercules in ancient times), skirting round the southernmost chunk of Iberia and passing what would later become the Algarve. He'd have then traveled up the coast, perhaps docking at Alcácer do Sal or carrying on as far as the port at Setúbal. Finally he would've reached Lisbon, through the sandbanks and upstream as far as the Mar da Palha mouth, where the river, still salty, flows into a small internal sea that may have reminded Ulysses of the Mediterranean. And before or after (but probably before) giving this delightful place his own name, Ulisseum, he would've sailed back down to Setúbal and Tróia, which back then, before silting changed the landscape, would still have been an island.

We imagined Ulysses exploring the region around Lisbon by land, reaching Sintra, going as far as Cabo da Roca (known to the Ancients as Ophiussa), Europe's westernmost point, and from there looking out over the Atlantic. He'd reached the end of the known world, the beginning of the great Sea of Darkness. It would have struck him as less blue than the Mediterranean, a strange and unfamiliar sea. Other sailors would one day cross the Atlantic, as well as the Indian and Pacific Oceans, and so twenty-four centuries after *The Odyssey* had been written, an adventurous poet by the name of Camões, embroiled in numerous Lisbon quarrels, would set out for Africa and Asia and have the nerve to put himself in Homer's place and write, off his own back, a new epic saga.

We too contemplated the Sea of Darkness, where we'd just been swimming. It was blue and calm, with little ripples that carried white foam towards the shore.

There we were, standing on the sunny beach in a place that for millennia had been called Tróia, imagining Ulysses' footprints in the sand like people hunting for dinosaur tracks. The difference being that dinosaurs had really existed; you could even see their fossilized footprints not far from where we were. But Ulysses' footprints had never existed and the only footprints in the sand were our own, for there was nobody else on the beach.

That same afternoon we went to visit the ruins at Tróia. We knew there had been a prosperous Roman village there from the first to the eleventh century AD. Its main occupations were salting fish and making garum, a popular sauce for banquets that was transported to Rome in huge amphorae.

The photos show you in denim shorts and a white T-shirt. In some of them you've removed your straw hat and your face, in close-up, is filled with light. There are even one or two photos of us together among the ruins, taken for us by another visitor, presumably an archaeologist (there illicitly, like us, since back then the ruins weren't open to the public).

There was one photo I particularly liked, which I enlarged several times and then stuck on the studio wall: it shows us hand in hand and strangely triumphant, advancing upon a devastated city.

That photo was the starting point for one of my paintings at the time: a very young man and woman walk among ruins without paying them the least attention. In contrast to the rubble that surrounds them (the city has been demolished), they're figures of joy, of affirmation, naked and amoral, a man and a woman demanding the right to be happy no matter the cost, defying the circumstances, the conventions of society and life, ready to face down all the galleons and armies of the world.

I called the painting *With Helen at Troy*.

Later on I made a sculpture with the same title, of a young couple kissing on the beach. (Tróia was deserted that April day, and we too made love on the beach.) The sculpture captures the moment when he leans over her, still half sitting to one side, but with their legs entwined and the water lapping at their feet. Her hair is spread over the sand.

The Odyssey was a timeless and universal tale. People would never stop telling it, could never stop telling it.

Ulysses' voyage was the story of all our lives; the whole of mankind could relate to him. Indeed the very first word in the book is "man."

It can be read as the first European novel, the source of all others that followed.

And the story has established itself in Lisbon's imagination like a second skin:

Ulysses sets off for war, for the sea, leaving his wife and child behind.

For centuries this has been Portugal's story too, women waiting at home alone, children growing up without fathers. It happened in the Crusades, the Age of Discovery, the colonial wars and times of emigration, right up until the end of the twentieth century.

And this doesn't only apply to the Homeric vulgate: even in its many other versions, the story could still easily be ours:

Penelope hears rumors of Ulysses' death and runs to drown herself in the sea. But she's saved by birds, probably gulls, which pull her back to shore;

Penelope tires of waiting for Ulysses and gives in to her suitors, especially one of them, Amphinomus. Ulysses learns of her affair with Amphinomus and comes back to kill her;

Ulysses returns to Ithaca, only to leave again, abandoning Penelope a second time, devastated by her infidelity;

Penelope tires of waiting for Ulysses and sleeps with all one hundred and twenty-nine of her suitors. From these liaisons the great god Pan is born;

But in not a single version of the story did Penelope choose one of her suitors to reign beside her as king of Ithaca;

And in no version did she become queen of Ithaca, taking on Ulysses' role, you might say. Although today, that's probably how the story would go.

Ulysses' absence (in the faithful version) robbed Penelope of her life, and Telemachus too, for he never had room to grow into a man. Ulysses took up all the space, as if he alone existed, even when he wasn't there. He alone was king. But twenty years later he was no longer king in his own right; he was the usurper, come to wrestle the throne from his son, who should in the meantime have got rid of Penelope's suitors and become king himself, with his own wife and child. This would have left no place for Ulysses when he returned, other than as one of his son's subjects.

But that version didn't exist either. Telemachus helped his father regain power, as if time had stood still. Ulysses insisted on controlling everything, ruling over everything, even time.

However, as it happened there was another version of the story, which seemed to have arisen in response to that one.

Ulysses was killed by his own son. Not by Telemachus, for Telemachus never grew up, but by Telegonus, the son of Ulysses and Circe. It is by Telegonus' hand that justice is done, for Ulysses' crime against Telemachus is unforgivable. (Although this version softens things by having this happen by accident.)

After killing Ulysses, Telegonus marries Penelope, his father's first wife, and Circe takes them both to the Islands of the Blessed.

We shared such tales on the beach at Tróia, our talk drifting wherever the wind took it. It was a conversation that seemed free and formless, but was (or would become) our story. Portugal's story, Lisbon's story.

Later that day I thought about other things, things I didn't tell you at the time:

Ulysses' story was about love between men and women, the homes they build, the perilous quest of making a life together. And the things men will say to recover their freedom.

In the Trojan War, Ulysses finds the perfect excuse to abandon Penelope. His wife, their son, and the island of Ithaca added up to too narrow a life, he was tired of daily domesticity and yearned to escape, to set off in search of adventure. He missed the manliness of war, a hard world without women. Not because he sought love and sex with another man, or men, as Achilles did, but because he felt suffocated by family life. Naturally he hid his desires behind typically masculine words: duty, honor, loyalty and all the rest of it. But the truth was, he wouldn't swap war for anything, and Troy was an irresistible prospect. There would of course be danger, traps, enemies, betrayals, deaths and shipwrecks, but he'd accept such risks if it meant being able to leave Penelope behind and set sail.

She wasn't enough for him. It wasn't her fault: no woman would ever have been enough for him. After all, she was his ideal woman, which is why he ended up favoring her over Helen, his initial choice. Instead of marrying Helen, Ulysses married Penelope, her more sensible but less beautiful cousin, who was nevertheless the daughter of a king, with all the financial advantages that entailed. Penelope was Ulysses' second choice, but a wise choice. Because Helen was too beautiful, too difficult to keep to his bed. Choosing Helen would've meant endlessly battling against the desires of other men who'd covet her the moment they laid eyes on her. Her looks made her too great a risk. But Penelope was plainer. She'd never behave like Helen, abandoning her husband and home to run away with a young lover to a foreign land. That was why Ulysses chose her.

But then he abandoned Penelope and left for Troy in search of Helen. Not for himself, he swore, but to return her to Sparta and her husband.

But it was Helen he was fighting for, it was for her that he devised the wooden horse and climbed inside its belly, it was for love of her that he opened the gates and let the city be destroyed. And afterwards it was Ulysses who defended Helen when the Greeks wanted to stone her to death, but before putting her on a ship and sending her back to Greece, he slipped away with her for an hour of love. Thus he fulfilled, albeit fleetingly, his desire: to make love to Helen. Only afterwards would he return to Penelope and the daily routine.

When I painted *With Helen at Troy*, everyone, from the gallery owner to the person who bought it, assumed the male figure was Paris. But I knew it was Ulysses, escaping with Helen to make love in the ruins of Troy. The sculpture I produced afterwards recorded the same moment in another form.

I'd picked out a few details here and there (Penelope, less beautiful than her cousin Helen, was indeed Ulysses' second choice in some retellings) but this myth is basically my own invention. And in no version of the story does Ulysses spend that hour with Helen at Troy.

More fortunate than Ulysses, I did have an hour of lovemaking at Troy. And to me you were Helen, Cecília, you were all women. If I were to paint you as them, you'd have the body of Circe, or the mermaids.

Mermaids. They formed part of Ulysses' universe and Lisbon's popular imagination. For instance there's a column featuring mermaids in the Madre de Deus church, and the mythology of fantastical sea beings is a recurring feature of our fifteenth- and sixteenth-century jewelry. Pliny the Elder, who came to Iberia in the first century, recounts that an ambassador was dispatched from Lisbon to inform the Emperor Tiberius that a merman had been seen in a grotto playing a conch shell. This most likely occurred in a cave near Colares that floods when the tide rises, according to Damião de Góis' sixteenth-century account. The waves crash and echo against the cave walls, making a sound so fierce "people still believe it to be the sound of the conch-playing merman once seen there."

Why send an ambassador to tell Tiberius? To make sure he was aware of how varied were his subjects? So that whoever captured the merman might be paid a reward?

These lines from an ancient document seemed to answer our questions: "And if by chance a whale or a whale-calf or *mermaid* or orca or dolphin or porpoise or any similar such giant fish should be killed in Sesimbra or Silves or other places belonging to the order of Santiago, then the king shall receive his due share."

They were fascinating stories, especially the accounts of mermaids, which had been common since ancient times across medieval and romance Europe. These legends were probably once based on sightings of monk seals and sea lions (*monachus monachus*), a species no longer found off our coasts but still common in Madeira. The sound they make is probably the famous song that seduced and led sailors astray.

Although, in a twelfth-century account by an English crusader who took part in the siege of Lisbon, the mermaids' song that reached him as his ship approached Iberia wasn't seductive in the slightest:

"We then heard the horrifying cry of the mermaids, which

sounded like weeping at first, then giggling and cackling, like a torrent of abuse from a village fair."

These fantastical sea creatures were said to take various forms. According to Damião de Gois, the ones that could still be found around Colares and Sintra no longer had fish tails, though they flaunted their scaly skin as "a vestige of their former race"; they'd jump out of the sea to steal fruit, which they were sometimes spotted greedily devouring, or to eat raw fish or warm themselves in the sun. It was said that at the approach of humans they'd throw themselves into the waves, either cackling with glee or screaming with fright.

Then there were stories like that of Dona Marinha, who was washed up on the shore, and the gentleman who fell in love with her, married her and had a child with her. She had no fish tail, and was equal or superior to land-dwelling women in every respect, even in her beauty—except for the fact she couldn't speak. Eventually despairing of her muteness, her husband ordered a bonfire be built and pretended their son had been thrown into the flames. Dona Marinha let out such a scream that a lump of flesh flew out of her mouth, setting her tongue free. From that point on she was able to speak, and was like a woman in every way. And they all lived happily ever after.

The sea was always bringing us strange creatures: mermaids who were fished onto the land, mermen or sea-men, and sea-women, extraordinarily beautiful varieties of mermaid, who men fell in love with.

Ambassadors were forever being dispatched from Lisbon, first to the Roman Emperor and later to the Popes, to inform them of the existence of creatures that had never been seen before.

What drew us to these legends was the tension, or clash, between two worlds. According to Damião de Gois, we captured sea-men in traps, and once they'd been tamed they adapted to a kind of domestic existence.

Which seems to mean we used them for our own ends, to serve us, or at least we liked to imagine we did. We probably thought removing them from their own environment and forcing them to live in ours was a perfectly normal thing to do, or even a "civilizing" act.

These fantastical stories anticipated what would happen later, with the sea voyages of the fifteenth century. We crossed oceans and found other creatures (not sea creatures, though they came to us from the sea, by means of the sea) that had never been encountered before. We learnt that despite everything we'd read in those ancient books, there were no headless creatures with eyes in their chests, or the heads of dogs, or a single foot so large that the rest of the body could hide in its shadow, and that carried it along at great speeds. Contrary to what had been written and believed since Antiquity, these beings didn't exist. But others did, beings of different colors and races, which to us seemed no less strange. There were "savages" who went around naked or semi-naked, their bodies covered in fur. They were "the other," different to us, and we found this disconcerting. Did they have souls? Were they human like us? How would we approach them? And what should we do with them?

Once again Lisbon dispatched ambassadors, this time to the Pope, so that he could interpret, understand, and define these beings for us. Were they savages, halfway between animals and humans? Or were they humans? And did they have souls?

The Pope decided they did have souls and therefore needed to be Christianized. To which end anything was acceptable, all methods could be justified as serving this higher purpose.

In fact, we exploited these human beings every chance we got, selling them as slaves and using them as forced labor. The Africans above all, for the Indians we considered less suited to work, and the Orientals had more weapons and defended themselves better.

In the fifteenth century Portugal and Spain were the

forerunners of maritime exploration, and with the Treaty of Tordesillas they rushed to divide the world up between them: half for you, half for me. Naturally, the Treaty fell apart as soon as other countries followed our example, learning our nautical techniques and then adding something we'd never had ourselves: formidable powers of organization. By the sixteenth century the English, Flemish and Dutch had entered the race, and the other European powers weren't far behind. Slavery spread throughout South and North America and lasted until the nineteenth century, with European colonialism extending well into the twentieth century. Portugal was the first country to trade in slaves and the last to relinquish its colonies. But it was also the first to officially abolish slavery (in Portugal and India in 1761, and in the rest of the empire in 1869) and a pioneer in abolishing the death penalty, which it did in 1867.

From the fifteenth century on, Europe considered itself superior to the rest of the world because Europeans had been the ones to cross seas and encounter other peoples and continents. Europe didn't care to realize it was threatening other people's existence, destroying their cultures, beliefs, and ways of seeing the world, nor did it consider giving them anything in exchange. Who was interested in exchanging things equitably? This was survival of the fittest—that is, of whoever had the best weapons and could seize the most wealth.

We Europeans were also wrong when we saw ourselves as the center of the world and everywhere else as the periphery. The world was round and so any part of it might be considered the center, depending on where you were standing: Europe, America, Africa, Asia.

But Eurocentrism seemed unquestionable then, because Europe was where the journey had begun, and history was written from a European point of view. Outside Europe there were only "the others" or "the other," very often written or spoken about, but never the ones writing or speaking.

In the centuries that followed, every European country that could became a colonizing power, and they all behaved the same way towards non-Europeans. There are no innocent Europeans in this story. And pretending that some were better than others is pure hypocrisy.

But five hundred years later, had the world really evolved? You hoped it had, I believed it hadn't. Exploitation and colonialism still existed in many forms, they were just subtler and more difficult to see. As a species, humans forever proved disappointing. And Lisbon happened to be a great place to reflect on these things.

Located on Europe's Western extreme, stuck between the Atlantic Ocean and the sometimes friendly, sometimes hostile Spain, Lisbon looked to the sea for a way out. And it found one. The verb *to depart* became part of us, a part that always wanted more and was never satisfied, that longed for what was out of reach.

We found it easy to imagine Lisbon dispatching and receiving goods, a port of passage. Assimilating the unfamiliar, adopting the exotic, the ex-optic—everything beyond what the eye could see.

New animals and plants were unveiled to a Europe obsessed with novelty, and went on to become part of the fabric of the city. Dürer made his famous woodcut of a rhinoceros after reading a letter describing the one Portugal was donating to the Pope. He later wrote in minute detail of an encounter with Portuguese merchants and traders on his second trip to Flanders, when they'd offered him three parrots. There is a small stone rhinoceros on a corner of the Belém Tower, and an unrealized design by Francisco de Holanda in the sixteenth century would've seen water shooting out of elephant trunks in a fountain in Rossio square. Via Lisbon and care of Portuguese ships, a profusion of rare and precious objects enriched the private collections of European courts in the sixteenth and seventeenth centuries. These *Kunst-und Wunderkammer*, cabinets of arts and curiosities, were a kind of living encyclopedia of the most unusual objects made by man or nature, put on display to be admired by distinguished guests and advertise their owner's erudition and wealth.

After successfully taking to the seas in the fifteenth and sixteenth centuries, Portugal became gripped by a sort of geo-maritime bulimia. A small country of no more than 35,000 square miles, with a population of one million in 1415 (which would drop to 900,000 by 1450), had placed stone crosses bearing the Portuguese coat of arms all over vast swathes of the planet as a symbol of its presence and rule. The occupied territory was often limited to the coastline, with little penetration inland, but the area explored was nevertheless immense, spanning the Atlantic, Indian, and Pacific Oceans. Titles declared Dom Manuel to be "the Lord of Guiné, in Africa, and conqueror and navigator of Ethiopia, Arabia, Persia and India"; the globe that featured on his coat of arms, so characteristic of the "Manueline" style, was a physical representation of his country's worldwide ambitions.

But the age of abundance, during which gold poured into Lisbon, lasted just sixty years: from the mid-fifteenth to the early sixteenth century. At the time, it seemed the ships would bring a never-ending supply of treasure: slaves, gold, spices, fabrics. The city flourished, filling with luxury and extravagance and becoming cosmopolitan. Representatives of Europe's most important banks and merchants flocked to it, sensing easy riches, as did spies from several countries, sniffing out information about trade routes and produce.

But incompetent leadership and excessive spending led the country to the brink of collapse. Despite ruling in times of peace and prosperity, both Dom João II and Dom Manuel left debts.

Other European nations began to compete with Portugal commercially and win. We weren't very good at managing or organizing ourselves, but we were highly skilled at bragging and squandering.

We had to close our trading post at Flanders, for example, and in 1549, we had our credit lines withdrawn in Antwerp and were forced to mortgage our future export revenues. In no time at all, interest rates doubled.

There was famine in Lisbon and grain had to be bought in Flanders at exorbitant rates, and even then there wasn't enough bread to go round. The country began to sell treasury bonds, postpone debt repayments and ask for more loans. We lived well beyond our means, and instead of generating our own wealth we tried to find it ready-made elsewhere. That's basically what we did with Africa and India.

The same thing happened again in the seventeenth and eighteenth centuries, with sugar, gold, and precious stones from Brazil: another period of apparent prosperity, yet more abundance lost. The country was forever fleeing into the future.

In 1557, Garcia de Resende lamented the lack of good government—something that would continually afflict us, and needlessly so.

We were forever gazing into the distance and neglecting what was right under our noses. With the country depopulated, we had neither the capacity nor the will to farm and fish, and the constant war effort was hugely costly, because expansion was always achieved by force. The "glory of ruling," as Camões once put it, soon descended into vanity and froth, and his great curmudgeon, The Old Man of Restelo, continued to be criticized and sneered at, but never listened to.

You and I, Cecília, always found it strange to think that Lisbon, even in such a violent period, also enjoyed times of tolerance in which different cultures and religions lived together peacefully side by side.

In the twelfth century, for example, three religions coexisted in Arabic Lisbon (then known as Al-Lixbuna): Muslims, Jews, and Christians all shared the same small space. This was deemed intolerable by European Christians and inspired English, German, and Dutch crusaders to join the first king of Portugal in his campaign to expand his small domain, which had only recently become a kingdom, further south:

"Given the huge agglomeration of men, there was no compulsory religion among the people; and because anyone could keep whatever religion they wanted, the most depraved men from all over the world were drawn there as to a sinkhole, making it a hotbed of licentiousness and filth," wrote the English crusader who recounted—in Latin—the siege of Lisbon. But in fact, those pure, holy crusaders, who claimed to be reinstating the Christian faith first introduced by the Romans centuries earlier, were principally driven by the desire to get rich by sacking the wealthy city, and they weren't disappointed. Their Christian faith didn't hold them back from committing atrocities, not even from decapitating the resident Christian bishop in order to replace him with an English one (a bishop was a valuable piece in those religious-political chess games, it was handy to have one of your own on a foreign board).

Despite all this, the Muslims who stayed on in the city afterwards were essentially afforded the same rights as Christians, so long as they paid their dues, just as the Christians had paid dues when it had been a Muslim city. Occupying themselves mostly with agriculture, the Muslims, or moors, lived in the Mouraria neighborhood, just as the Jews lived in the Judiaria, or Jewry. Despite the separate districts, there continued to be relative tolerance throughout the Middle Ages, and it was thanks to this that the city prospered in the centuries that followed. The cultural and scientific progress that enabled the great sea voyages to take place, and was the genuinely positive side of the Age of Discovery, marked the continuation of work begun centuries before by Arabs and Jews. They'll always be a part of Portugal's rich cultural heritage.

From a scientific and technological point of view, the great sea voyages of the fifteenth century signified a huge leap forward. They required major developments in mathematics, the nautical sciences, sail mechanics and ship design, and an understanding of how to navigate in another hemisphere, using different constellations. At that time, Portugal wrote treatises on shipbuilding; perfected their vessels in shipyards outside Lisbon; opened the first cartography school; worked out how to make precise calculations of latitude, which were then added as a scale to sixteenth-century naval charts, along with approximations of longitude (longitude wasn't calculated with any precision until the eighteenth century). New knowledge was acquired in zoology, botany, medicine, pharmacology, linguistics, ethnology and geology. Portugal was not alone in these endeavors, but our role cannot be overlooked.

Yet very few people in Portugal, let alone the rest of the world, have ever heard of the 1915 *Oriental Summary* by Tomé Pires, for example, or *Colloquies on the Simples & Drugs of India* by Garcia de Orta, the mathematics books of Pedro Nunes, the Tupi grammar books of Padre Anchieta, or the *Pilgrimage* by Fernão Mendes Pinto, so modern that it views our maritime saga with a degree of distance and questions—this, as long ago as the sixteenth century—the relationship between servant and master.

How many people have read our travel books, which helped to change the way the world was seen? And how many realize we've existed as a country since 1143, with the same borders since 1297?

In Portugal, however, tolerance was always intermittent. Muslims and Jews were the victims of persecution between 1496 and 1498, and in 1506 two thousand Jews were massacred outside the São Domingos church in Lisbon. And from 1536 to 1821 there was the Inquisition, which spread into Portugal from Spain.

The first "autos-da-fé" took place in 1540, and they remained popular spectacles until as late as the eighteenth century, attracting huge audiences to the Terreiro do Paço and Rossio squares.

These are painful truths. History (for Portugal and for the world) seemed always to consist of tiny steps forward and giant steps back.

There were many good beginnings: the first public courts date back to 1254, and the first university opened in 1290.

But we could never rid ourselves of a tendency towards oligarchy and absolute rule. In the golden era of Dom Manuel, the courts were only convened three times in his twenty-five-year reign. Absolutism held until 1834, only for a forty-eight-year dictatorship to begin less than a hundred years later.

And since the sixteenth century, our public accounts have almost never been in credit. With the very rare and brief exception, we were only ever consistently in the black under the dictatorship, at the cost of immense suffering and tremendous atrophy in other areas.

In the decrepit Pátio dos Quintalinhos courtyard, on Rua das Escolas Gerais, there's nothing to mark the site of the first university. Our cultural and architectural heritage are victims of continual neglect.

We lived in Graça, a working-class neighborhood full of tiny cafés, grocery stores, fruit and veg shops and friendly neighbors. (Some of them famous, like the artist Maria Keil or the writer Sophia de Mello Breyner, who loved Greece as much as we did and lived just around the corner, on Travessa das Mónicas.) The location was also very convenient: just a brief stroll and you were in different neighborhoods: Mouraria, Alfama, Castelo, Baixa.

It was the sort of place where you could pop into the bakery for a loaf of bread still warm from the oven, and be on a first name basis with the waiters in the café, who hurried between tables balancing precarious trays and shouting orders back to the counter: "Another *bica* coffee!"

Or speak to strangers in the queue at the grocer's or waiting at the bus stop; say "Isn't it cold today?" without it being interpreted as a sexual advance or a sign of madness.

I visited the former workers' villages with you, Cecília; Vila Berta with its wrought-iron verandas covered in flowers, Vila Maria, and Vila Sousa, where I told you *O Pátio das Cantigas* had been filmed and showed you the street lamp from the famous scene.

You liked the little shops, the cafés, the San Giorgio tailor's, with its floor paved black and white like the street outside, its windows adorned in white. And I remember when you became interested in the Estrela de Ouro workers' village and Agapito, the boss whose name was plastered across the factory façade in giant letters and who named streets after his wife and daughters, Josefa Maria, Rosalina and Virgínia. This Agapito character fascinated you. You thought his conspicuous use of his own name probably had something to do with his humble Galician roots; perhaps he wanted to use his own success to avenge the centuries of hardship suffered by his compatriots. Galicians had long wandered the streets of Lisbon bent double under water barrels, sacks of produce or luggage, as if it were every Galician's destiny to be a beast of burden having come here dreaming of a brighter future, believing that he who dreams gets, even if all you get is a kick in the guts, and a good kick in the guts was often all they did get. But Agapito stuck two fingers up to such a fate, he owned a cake factory and a patisserie in Baixa, both called Estrela de Ouro, Golden Star, which was what he called everything he owned, perhaps to show he was born under a lucky one (although the star symbol was more likely masonic— something you always planned to investigate). He built an entire neighborhood for his workers in the early twentieth century, hearths and homes for 120 families, and for himself a house with a garden and a chapel. Set apart from the workers' village, I pointed out, but you thought that in Portugal, where corruption raged and colossal fortunes were made in secret, it wasn't socially acceptable to live alongside your workers and put the rewards of your efforts on public display.

The boss, one way or another, was always the villain of the piece, because envy was a national disease. So you read up on Agapito, looked into how he made his fortune, how much he paid his workers, how much the rent was on their homes, which were by no means poorhouses, and indeed many years later would become much sought-after by the middle classes. Nor was Agapito's own residence especially over the top; it wasn't a palace or a mansion, just a decent-sized house with a garden and a courtyard. And although the stone pond may have been in poor taste, it was to Agapito's taste at least and did no harm to anyone, any more than his chapel did. He may not have been very well spoken, his grammar may not always have been correct, but he did more to promote culture in the city than many of our eloquent, intellectual ministers ever have. He built a cinema in the neighborhood, the Royal (sadly now turned into a supermarket), which the workers would go to as well (let's check, you said, whether they got a discount). It was here that the first sound film was ever shown in Portugal, and the screening was attended by the President of the Republic—who almost certainly didn't pay for his ticket, or even so much as break an egg into one of Agapito's cakes.

Everything but the moo, as they say, and Agapito certainly threw little away and made the most of what he had. Starting with his own background, which you planned to find out more about so that it might become an example to others.

Workers' struggles mattered to you too, of course, and you'd think of them whenever you passed the house of the labor leader

Angelina Vidal, or the Voz do Operário social welfare society. But these fights weren't against the Agapitos of this world, or at least you didn't think they were.

In the end, though, you never did research Agapito's story. Information was hard to come by; it seemed nobody had ever taken much of an interest in him, and besides, you weren't a sociologist or historian. We never spoke of him again, or of the industrialists in other neighborhoods, or of an earlier businessman you'd come across in the Madre de Deus museum, whose story had been told in ceramics. He referred to himself as "the Mister," which immediately sparked your curiosity, and had been a genuine self-made man, starting from nowhere, working hard all his life and eventually setting up a small ceramics factory of his own. But nobody seemed to care about these stories anymore.

In Portugal, wealth was wasted on unproductive goods; for centuries the kings and aristocracy had traded and frittered all proceeds away. In Lisbon and its surrounds there was an array of royal palaces and an impressive number of villas, some extremely beautiful, which almost always proved ill-suited to other uses and in many cases were left to ruin.

You said churches were sad and statues of saints reminded you of ghosts, with their faded satin shawls and tortured expressions. Not to mention the Stations of the Cross, a statue in the church just down from where we lived; Jesus bent under the weight of the crucifix, with his crown of thorns, long hair and pale face. Or St. Justine in her glass coffin in the Church of Saint Anthony, looking as if her body had just been exhumed. You hated this taste for suffering and the macabre, the reliquaries containing shards of skull and bone, the memento mori. I told you that in times gone by, Lisbon used to display dead bodies outside the São João de Deus convent on the Day of the Dead, propping them up against the wall and adorning them with laurel branches. I also described the ritual digging up of bones that used to take place, and the street altars assembled by the Brotherhood of Souls.

But you'd just burst out laughing and refuse to go into any churches. Yes, you said, they may be opulent and beautiful, whether Roman, Gothic, or Neo-classical, but who was this show of wealth for? And besides, there were too many of them; it would surely be impossible to find anywhere with more churches per square meter than the center of Lisbon.

You preferred open spaces, parks in particular. Like the garden near us with its little Flora statue and modest round pond, elderly locals sitting on benches in the morning sun, mothers out with their children, and that beautiful view of the city.

"City of Ulysses," we used to say. But we used the phrase in a vague, all-encompassing way, as a sort of umbrella term for everything we wanted to say about Lisbon. Which was whatever we happened to find interesting about it, simple as that.

Lisbon was the sort of place where you had to look out for what couldn't be seen as well as what could—what had once been there but was now gone. It was a place for people who liked digging around and finding things out, and who were happy to do a little background work beforehand. A city to conquer, to unearth little by little and find out what lay beneath the surface, the different layers of time.

(To learn, for example, that the river Tagus used to reach as far as the Rua dos Bacalhoeiros and crash against the city walls and that the city extended alongside its quays and beaches; that two streams used to meet in what is now Praça da Figueira, one coming down from the Arroios valley, the other from the Santo Antão valley; that the watercourses still reveal themselves in lower-lying streets, such as Regueirão dos Anjos, that the city's grandest boulevard, Avenida da Liberdade, once divided the vegetable gardens of São José and Valverde, both long gone. That the Arco do Cego and Benfica neighborhoods used to be summer retreats; the Dona Maria National theater stands on what was once the site of the Estaus Palace, headquarters of the Inquisition, in Rossio square; the Cerca Moura, Lisbon's former defensive wall, dates back to Swabian or Visgothic times; the Hospital de Todos os Santos used to be in Praça da Figueira; and the Arco Escuro tunnel in Alfama was once a sea gateway.)

As we wandered through the streets our eyes would fall upon details; verandas, windows, kiosks, corners, gables, fountains, signs with curious names. It was a city in which an unexpected place, scene, or feature waited around every corner. A tiny city made of tiny things. But it was also a kaleidoscope, forming new patterns with every shift in perspective: there was spiritual Lisbon, for example, including the cult (outlawed under the dictatorship) that surrounds the statue of the spiritist Dr. Sousa Martins, before which candles, flowers, offerings, memorial stones, and photographs are placed; and other secret, mysterious Lisbons, forests of symbols, Masonic and others; an esoteric city in which enigmatic figures stare out from the background of paintings, the Lisbon of the São Vicente panels, in which things can be seen that almost certainly aren't there, but that stir the imagination and ingenuity of anyone who looks at them. But we didn't follow that particular trail. We left the secret, occult, and magical to the likes of Pessoa; there were special walking routes for anyone into such things, guided tours, though the truly initiated, like Pessoa, preferred to go their own way, be their own masters.

(I remember, for example, us wondering whether Damião de Gois' description of Lisbon being "a city shaped like the bladder of a fish when viewed from Almada" was simply a banal and prosaic comparison or a veiled reference to "vesica piscis," a geometric figure with a long symbolic tradition, the name of which meant "fish bladder" in Latin. But we didn't follow that trail either; it seemed to lead into a huge labyrinth, from which there was probably no escape.)

And yet we were drawn to the labyrinth. Seen from above, Lisbon spread out like a great maze, and there were plenty of up-above places to see it from, not least the Graça and Senhora do Monte viewpoints near our house. There were beautiful, expansive views from both, but also the disconcerting sense that thousands of invisible eyes might be watching you from behind the thousands of windows. Equally disconcerting was the false sense of perspective, for whereas a view of a flat surface gives you a feeling of security, Lisbon was like an optical illusion: rooftops that appeared to be joined together were in fact separated by roads, and houses that looked to be side by side in reality had alleyways, arches, steps, passages, and courtyards tucked in between them. When you looked out upon it, broken lines cut through your gaze, defying you, tricking you. To begin unraveling the ball of wool we had to walk down each street on foot, one at a time, taking care not to get tangled up ourselves as we went. Because it was easy to lose track of the irregular patterns of streets that suddenly stopped, overlapped or changed direction, only to lead to a dead end. In the old town, the only certainty was that if you headed downwards, one way or another you'd end up in Baixa or at the river, regardless of how many false turns you took along the way.

And it was curious to see the play of perspectives between one viewpoint and another; whether they complemented or contradicted each other. I remember how you liked to station yourself in the highest places in the city and draw, tracing the dialogue between one viewpoint and another: the Graça viewpoint seen from the Senhora do Monte viewpoint and vice versa; Graça and Senhora do Monte seen from the São Pedro de Alcântara viewpoint, and São Pedro de Alcântara seen from either of them; the view from the castle to Senhora do Monte via Graça, and back to the castle from Senhora do Monte.

Lisbon was a city of broken lines and splintered perspectives. Everything was in pieces, and it took patience to fit it all back together again. And there would always be a few bits missing; walking around revealed hidden gaps, interruptions, ruptures.

We uncovered a collection of broken fragments, the remains of cities built one on top of the other, from periods and civilizations that had each reached a certain juncture and disappeared. Not without leaving their mark.

Thus the city had grown vertically upwards from the subsoil, and you could see signs of this at archaeological sites and in museums, evidence of indigenous cultures, statues of gods like Endovelicus, remains of Phoenician, Roman and Visgothic settlements, and numerous traces of the Arabic city. But you could see it too in the city itself; the Roman theater, for example, was relatively near to us, on Rua da Saudade, right beneath the poet Ary dos Santos' house.

There were even a few houses still standing from before the 1755 earthquake, after which the center of Lisbon was rebuilt according to the vision of the Marquis of Pombal.

Another Lisbon was made up of horizontal sections laid out side-by-side, expanding outwards over fields and vegetable gardens, trampling on streams and stifling rivers with landfill. The city had expanded as a series of villages became stuck together, swallowing up the fields in between. It made for a curious juxtaposition, with the cosmopolitan brushing up against the provincial until well into the twentieth century. I remember telling you, for instance, about the livestock that used to graze beside an apartment block in Lumiar as late as 1975, and that I even once saw a sheep being born there. (I'd been visiting a friend, Orlando, and as I left his building I suddenly found myself in the middle of a passing flock, but something had made them slow down, and when I looked back I saw the shepherd had stopped. I made my way through the animals towards him and saw that a lamb was giving birth. I watched, somewhat alarmed, for I'd never seen an animal being born before. When it was over, the shepherd picked up the newborn lamb and slung it over his shoulder like a rabbit, the head and two legs at the front, the rest of the body and the back legs dangling behind. The mother sheep hauled herself to her feet and staggered a few steps, then recovered her poise and trotted alongside the shepherd and her baby lamb. It had all happened so fast and so naturally, there was no reason for me to have been alarmed. Nor was there anything alarming about there being green pastures right in the middle of the city, next to apartment blocks that didn't even have sidewalks leading to them. It was simply how Lisbon was.)

You liked this idea of the patchwork city, separate pieces joined in an overarching structure. It seemed to reflect the way decorative tiles combined to make a whole. You were very fond of tiles, lace, and rugs, particularly their tessellation, the notion of joining together single segments or threads until overall motifs emerged: a pattern (whether geometric or not), a figure, a scene, a narrative, a demarcated story, standing out against a neutral or empty background. These neutral, empty pieces were key, for they gave everything else emphasis and enabled the design to take shape. Just like life, for life was made of connected fragments, some of them empty, some of them full.

It was around that time that you made a series of artworks using squares of paper the size of tiles and employing a range of techniques. You made them into compositions, arranged with empty spaces in between.

I remember you liked to experiment with different materials, to paint on fabric or linen, enjoying the contrasting textures. You made several tapestry design cards and you were fascinated by collage, which was another way of uniting disparate pieces, fragments.

Going back to fantastical beings and the difficulty the world evidently has accepting other people's realities, I told you about various books I'd come across in Germany from the sixteenth century (by Franck, Muenster, Elucidarius, Schultes, and others), which I'd found very entertaining. They told of the strange creatures that Herodotus, Pliny, Ptolemy, etc. had described in ancient times, and for two centuries they were widely read and much admired. Their authors pondered whether Africans were human or not, and described troglodytes who lived in holes underground, headless Garamantes and one-eyed Cyclops.

In the Renaissance, people found it difficult to question the classics, to challenge the ancients and themselves in light of the new world taking shape around them. Sometimes reality itself had to be distorted, to prevent it from clashing with what they thought they knew. There was as much resistance to breaking down these barriers as there was to casting doubt on the Bible or acknowledging Galileo's observations. For example, Hartmann Schedel said in his illustrated essay that "the King of Portugal's voyages discovered people with dogs' heads and ears as long as a donkey's; their bodies had normal arms and hands, but their thighs and backsides were those of a horse; and they chewed like a cow." In fact, this description never appeared in any Portuguese texts. But how could they accept what was really happening? It was difficult to dismiss myths, to doubt the classics, and it was especially difficult to consider divine creation in a new way. Had the strange beings from faraway places also been made by God? How was this possible, if we were the creatures made in God's image? Could it be that God had various images? Or were these strange beings creations not of God but of (the dreaded word, terrifying even to utter) the Devil?

I remember how interesting you found people's resistance to recognizing and accepting the Other. You took to drawing monstrous figures based on the beings I described to you; beasts with four arms, four eyes, a dog's head, one foot, one eye, no head, and eyes at the chest.

You tried to trace how that way of seeing the world had transformed over time into the modern understanding that the other was not a monster, that it made no sense to demonize them because they were exactly the same as us.

But had we ever fully accepted this? I'd ask. Had the world ever truly decided that breeding only mattered in relation to animals like dogs and horses, and that among people there was only one race that counted, the human race?

I remember you going to the Museum of Ancient Art to copy, as an exercise, a Portuguese painting of Hell by an anonymous artist, dated between 1510 and 1520, which depicted the Devil as an indigenous Brazilian. The painting intrigued you. Although Portuguese explorers had encountered real, flesh-and-blood indigenous people in Brazil as long ago as 1500, we continued to see them as hybrid creatures, with women's breasts, a man's sex and an animal's tail, scales at the shoulders like a dragon, claws for hands and horns sprouting from their heads.

You also drew plant species on small pieces of card, as if seeing them for the first time. The pepper plant, the dragon tree (common in Madeira, and from which "dragon's blood" was extracted), the cinnamon tree, ginger, cloves. Exotic animals, too, which came to you like apparitions or revelations: elephants, rhinos, zebras, civets, tigers, lions, monkeys, jaguars, parrots, birds of paradise. And the valuable or rare objects that Lisbon supplied to all of Europe: Seychelles coconuts, ostrich eggs, rhinoceros horns, elephant teeth.

Another tradition we sometimes enjoyed exploring was puppetry shows, which really took off in Lisbon in the eighteenth century. Marionettes and doll puppets of various kinds delighted audiences at Pátio das Arcas, the city's first playhouse, at the Puppet Theater itself, and even sometimes at the opera house (Tagus Opera House, a huge building, which had been open just a few months when the earthquake struck and razed it to the ground).

We thought it was time for the tradition to make a comeback. And so it did, if only in our heads. We imagined eighteenth-century puppet shows being rewritten, reinvented and performed in Lisbon once more, alongside episodes from the Inquisition trials—the trial of Damião de Gois, perhaps, which so captivated Lisbon—to remind us all how unfair the law can be, and how far fanaticism and fundamentalism can go. We'd replicate the sense of theater, the pomp and circumstance, the display of power, the whole Baroque staging, which was a spectacle in itself. Carlos Seixas, Marcos Portugal, Bomtempo, and others would provide the soundtrack; seemingly light music to contrast with the barbaric scenes. We'd perform comic plays by António José da Silva, known as The Jew, alongside scenes from the trial that condemned him to death. We'd show how there was an auto-da-fé in Rossio square every two years, to educate the masses and make God's judgment shine bright. It didn't matter if it was God's judgment or the Devil's, nor whether the Holy Inquisition was more diabolical than it was saintly, so long as people knelt and did what they were told. The King stood above everything and his power was absolute—although he was beneath God, of course. But God delegated responsibilities to the Church, the Inquisition and the King, and all three of them pretended to be God. It was all theater, all pretend. Artifice, optical illusions and false perspectives. You had to pretend if you wanted to survive, so everyone pretended: that they'd converted, that they were rich or poor, that they helped the needy, that they fasted and wore a hair shirt. That they were good and chaste; honest; virgins. The baroque splendor of lying, the trompe l'oeil, the optical illusion, the stage sets and tricks of the light.

And yet in the midst of this all-consuming theater and pretense, the violence was real and the pain of those tortured or burnt alive was real. They were the flames of the candles, the fireworks that lit up the show.

But in the City of Ulysses, it was to Ulysses we always returned in the end.

Rome had shaped Lisbon and left indelible marks on the city, not least in terms of language. But Roman civilization did not bequeath a book like *The Odyssey*, nor philosophical concepts that would change the world for ever, like Rationality and Democracy. Hellenic civilization was the highest point European cultural thought had ever reached. That's why we kept going back to it. Searching for roots.

And that's why we found the figure of Ulysses so compelling: through him, we felt somehow connected to those concepts, rationality and democracy. Neither here nor anywhere else had they truly ever been adopted or practiced—and yet how desperately we needed them.

In fact, *The Odyssey* was written in the eighth century BC, some three centuries before these concepts emerged (and it harked back to an even more ancient time: the fall of Troy would have been in 1215 BC). But in our imagination, Ulysses represented the Hellenic legacy. He'd left his own bygone age, his island of shepherds and sailors, and journeyed through time to bring us the three fundamental things the Greeks had given the world: Rationality, Democracy, and *The Odyssey*.

That, we thought, was why the myth of Ulysses proved so enduring.

Over millennia, these concepts spread and made deep impressions. However many times they were trampled upon or snuffed out, they proved resistant and emerged reborn. Although they'd never properly existed anywhere in the world. Imperfect approximations were the best that could be found.

And Lisbon was the ideal place to reflect on these things.

Meanwhile, we realized we were not alone in our search for Lisbon. We found a remarkable number of people who'd loved the city before we did, studying, researching, painting, photographing, recording, filming, discussing and interpreting it for themselves. Our vision bore a debt to all of them, from the inevitable big names to the journalists who penned short pieces about this and that, and even ordinary residents who, attentive and determined to speak their mind, wrote letters to the city's newspapers. Yes, we were just two among a huge number of others.

It became clear that citizens had forever been engaged in a battle with the destructive forces of private interests. We'd have lost far more of the city's heritage than we already had were it not for the strength of public feeling, which, despite everything, still carried some weight. No matter what period we turned to, we always came across some outrage that the undersigned had railed against, like fire fighters committed to putting out one blaze after the next. Sadly, often without success.

In Martim Moniz, for example, a section of lower Mouraria has been destroyed and will never be recovered. We have lost countless historical cafés: in Rossio, Pessoa's beloved Brasileira; the Chave d'Ouro, which vanished in 1959; or the Colombo patisserie, which was recently replaced by a McDonald's. And back then we'd never have believed that, in the year 2000, a Roman cemetery and eleventh-century Islamic neighborhood would be condemned to the subsoil of Praça da Figueira to make way for a car park.

The examples, had we attempted to list them all, would've gone on forever.

But what, ultimately, would we choose to include in an exhibition about Lisbon?

Well, there was no need to be methodical or exhaustive, to follow a chronological order or indeed any kind of order at all. We could be dizzying and synchronous, overlap time frames, provide a partial, interrupted and even chaotic vision—and indeed that was all it could ever be, for it would entirely depend on us and our fragmentary impressions of the city.

If it were ever to exist, it would be an exhibition-performance, a multimedia experience, spread across a labyrinthine arrangement of rooms through which visitors could wander, choosing a route or surrendering to chance. Lisbon would be something that happened to them. There would therefore be many ways through it; no two visitors would come out having seen the same thing. And it would be almost impossible to see it all, without coming back several times. There would be a plethora of objects, maps, photos, slides, videos, films. Puppeteers would summon visitors, draw them into the show, produce marionettes from a bag and suddenly bring them to life, string puppets would appear, sometimes mingling with actors in the Lisbon theater tradition. And there would be puppet shows and operas, possibly in miniature, with stage props from the eighteenth century.

One area of the exhibition would be marked with a sign: Warning! Mind the Gap!

It would have safety railings around it for people to hold onto. Whenever anyone entered the area, which would be as narrow as a corridor and require visitors to go in single file, the ground would suddenly drop ten to fifteen inches, and for a few seconds people would feel as if the floor had given way. And in the moment when they reached for the railings and looked down at their feet, afraid they were falling, the words

CORRUPTION!

WARNING! MIND THE GAP!

would appear before them in giant letters, projected onto the floor and all the surrounding walls.

This would make people laugh afterwards, or else infuriate them. It would be a brief comic episode, or possibly a very irritating one, but either way it would stick in their memory, even if they didn't want it to, and so would the message. An exhibition could or should be an experience. Wasn't the purpose of works of art, and by extension the galleries that exhibited them, not just to provide pleasure, information and entertainment, but also to provoke reflection, transformation and change?

And in some, if not all the rooms, deconstructed fado music would play in the background. Deconstructed in the sense that no one fado song would ever be recognizable, there would merely be the suggestion of guitars and a voice, sensed more than heard, present in a subtle, subliminal way. From time to time the volume would increase and a phrase would become almost audible, only to then disappear again, like a wave washing onto the beach and vanishing in the sand.

(Fado was not melancholic, you used to say. It was proud.)

And there would be—

And there would be—

And there would be—

But we wouldn't ever put on this exhibition, it was just an excuse to laugh and talk nonsense.

Still, every once in a while we'd come back to the idea.

Lisbon was everywhere we looked, impossible to ignore, tripping us up at every step.

It was the ground we walked on. And because it was where we'd met and fallen in love, it belonged to us.

But, deep down, it wasn't Lisbon we were trying to find; we were trying to find each other and ourselves within it. We were travelers, and travelers' paths always lead back to themselves. Travelers want to understand who they are and where they're from. And as Novalis once wrote, we're always really going home.

Our vision of the city was part of ourselves and our story. We were the point of view.

And so the time has come to talk about us, Cecília. Having gone in search of Lisbon with you, I must now go in search of us, look at us. From very close quarters.

3.
In Search of Ourselves

We were very different people, almost total opposites in some ways, like light and shadow.

You came from a different country, for a start. You were born in Mozambique in 1964. In 1974 you were ten, and the fact there was a revolution taking place in Portugal meant nothing to you. Portugal was just a colored shape with a black outline on a giant map of the world, like everywhere outside Africa.

Africa was the only world you knew, and you'd been happy there. You'd even had a pet lion cub, which your father and his friends had brought back from a hunting trip one day. I forget the details, but for some reason or other the lion cub was lost when they saw him—maybe his mother had died—and he was so hungry he let himself be caught. For three weeks he lived in your house, drinking milk and playing in the yard like any other small domestic animal. And even though you knew there was no other choice, you were most upset when the time came for you and your parents to take him to the Gorongosa nature reserve and release him back into the semi-wild.

I remember all the things you used to tell me about; the tropical climate, the beaches, the bush, the varieties of tree we didn't have here, the immensity of the landscape. Yes, there had also been colonialism and war, and these days you saw your childhood memories in a different light. But you always maintained that what mattered most in Portugal's relationship with Africa was not politics but encounters between individual people. Many migrants went out there because they were struggling to survive at home, you used to say. Most people didn't behave like colonizers or feel superior to Africans, so you said; they were simply poor people in search of a better life, and as time passed, the different populations integrated more, and it wasn't unusual for families to have an African cousin, uncle, aunt, grandparent or brother- or sister-in-law. Nobody would bat an eyelid; it was considered perfectly normal. Your experience of primary school had been a happy one too, with black and white children mixing easily together.

You spoke too of the dialogue between cultures, the reciprocal influences and cross-pollination. None of this could be measured, and none of it had anything to do with trade and the financial markets. But it was ultimately what counted, real experiences, life as it was lived.

When you came to Lisbon for the first time, towards the end of 1974, you were quite unaware of colonialism, war, revolution, and all the other problems of the time. You arrived by boat with your mother (your father would follow later), and you remembered passing the Bugio lighthouse, the Belém Tower, the red bridge over the Tagus, the built-up areas on either riverbank, and staring curiously at this unfamiliar city. You could still picture yourself, aged ten, leaning over the deck, on the threshold of another continent.

You'd been at sea for days on end. As the ship made its way from the Indian Ocean into the Atlantic, you'd slept in a cabin, sat in the lounges, and played on deck with the other children, meeting officers and sailors who told you tales of travel and ships.

Life on board was repetitive and yet constantly new. You were interested in everything, always hoping to discover something unexpected when you looked out of a porthole. On some days the ship anchored in some port or other and you were able to go ashore, and on others you saw nothing but waves, seagulls, ships in the distance and water flecked with white foam.

Lisbon, where the ship finally docked, was at the end of two oceans. Or the beginning. It was a place of arrival and departure, an open city. Inclining over a river that carried it out to sea.

And when you were taken on trips to Estoril, Cascais, or Guincho, the ocean was always in sight, following you along the coastline. In and around Lisbon, everywhere led to the sea. The continents were linked by vast bodies of water, and you could reach the end of the world in a boat. You'd made this discovery on your maritime adventure, your first sea voyage. Lisbon had many other places within it, because the vast blue of the sea promised them.

You knew there were other worlds—you'd seen them with your own eyes. Africa, the Indian Ocean, savannahs, waterfalls, forests, wild animals, hot beaches, baobabs, tropical landscapes. You'd never forget them, could never forget them. They were written into your skin like a tattoo.

You spent a few months with relatives in Estoril, and then moved to England with your parents. Your father, an engineer and previously a university professor in the capital of Mozambique, then known as Lourenço Marques, had found a job with a company in London.

Oddly enough, you'd felt at home in Lisbon. It reminded you of Lourenço Marques in many ways. London, on the other hand, seemed alien, and was never a place you wanted to settle. And so eight years later you found yourself back in Lisbon, enrolled as a student at the School of Fine Arts, though in London the Slade School had been right on your doorstep.

To my surprise, your parents had let you decide for yourself where to study, making no attempt to convince you that returning to Lisbon was a ridiculous idea. Probably (but this is just my theory), they thought the Slade mattered less than your sense of identity and belonging. If London seemed foreign to you and holidays to Lisbon always felt like coming home, it made sense for you to leave England. The Slade could wait until another time.

It seemed to me that your relationship with Lisbon was colored by the circumstances in which you'd arrived to study. It'd been your choice to move there. You could explore the city from a privileged position, as both insider and outsider: you could accept it or reject it. I sometimes felt overwhelmed by how much you'd seen in your life: you'd crossed an ocean to get here. And although you'd always felt like an outsider in London, your eight years there had given you a broader European perspective.

There were many other things about you I found extraordinary. You were so very young, but at the same time so very mature, and in ways that often took me by surprise. Later, I came to attribute this to your African side. Women there grow up early and take easily to love.

Anyone who has ever lived in Africa leaves a part of themselves there, you used to say. And even if they never go back for it, or maybe because they never do, they'll dream about it forever.

Your parents married very young and moved to Lourenço Marques soon afterwards. When you were born, your mother was twenty-two and your father twenty-three. Your parents and mine were a generation apart, and they belonged to different worlds.

Your parents loved each other and were happy, you said. I often thought that seeing love up close, through them, must be what had made you so self-assured and strong. And that it was because your parents were happy themselves that they allowed you so much freedom and trusted your instincts.

When you told them you'd moved in with me, they increased your monthly allowance, no questions asked. If you'd chosen me, then what could they do but approve? They had faith in your ability to know what was best. Or perhaps they believed life was about trial and error, and you had to make your own mistakes. Whatever it was, I was struck by how easily everything happened on your side.

On my side, there wasn't much to tell. I was at the Lisbon
School of Fine Arts in 1974 and '75. In 1976 I received a
German grant to study in Berlin, at the Hochschule der Künste
in Wilmersdorf, and remained in Berlin until 1980. As soon as I
arrived I knew I wanted to stay longer, and I knew my grant, at
best, would only be extended (as indeed it was) for another year.
So right from the start I worked evenings and weekends and
saved money. I took on whatever jobs came along, washing cars,
delivering newspapers at dawn, scrubbing dishes and waiting
tables in restaurants and cafes, and accumulated enough money
to carry on studying beyond the grant. In the holidays, I put a
rucksack on my back and traveled around Europe, hitch-hiking
or inter-railing. I visited what I considered to be the most
important countries and galleries in Europe for the fine arts. I
was free and self-sufficient, and it felt good.

When you met me, I was living on my own in Lisbon and
answered to anybody.

I liked listening to you, but I didn't like talking about myself.
Especially not about my childhood, which I generally tried to
forget. Your childhood had been filled with light, whereas mine
was too dark to be spoken of.

Everything I told you was perfectly true, but it wasn't the
whole story:

My father, Sidónio Ramos, was an army officer who had
just been promoted to major when he met my mother. He
was a widower, his first wife having died young and without
bearing any children. When I was born, he was forty-four, my
mother twenty-eight. I always painted her in a good light when
I described her to you, and not only because she was young and
pretty.

My father was a brusque, irritable man, and he imposed
military discipline on our home in the form of short, sharp
orders that were to be immediately obeyed. He was methodical

and organized, and to him being a husband and father meant managing a small, conventional world that had strict rules and routines and was safeguarded by a modest bank account, which had to register an increase every month, even if it was only a small one. I think that's more or less what I told you. And I explained that not only did my father and I fundamentally disagree on almost everything, he also refused to understand or accept that I wanted to become an artist.

I didn't tell you that he'd been longing for a child since well before I was born. I'd come late in his life, and he'd placed all his hopes in me. But he felt I'd failed him, and made this very clear.

For years, my feelings in relation to him were essentially fear, confusion, and shame.

Growing up, I had very little interest in toy guns and plastic soldiers. I had even less interest in the real gun he once showed me, which, though unloaded, shocked and even frightened me. In other words, I never belonged to his world. We both knew it and it created a barrier between us. If his son, so longed for and, I still believe, so loved, had nothing in common with him, then why did the boy even exist? Why wasn't he like his father, built in his image?

Why wasn't he interested in horses, hunting, and pellet guns like any other boy?

I remember one day, at our farmhouse in Beira where we spent the summers, he showed up outside riding a horse and made it go up the steps of the raised shed where we kept the firewood. The horse hesitated, because horses understand danger and hate going up steps almost as much as they hate going down them. But it did what it was told.

I had to do what I was told too. Like the horse. It was that or stand up to that tempestuous man once and for all, that army major who had appeared on a horse and made it do strange things against its will. But I was so young, so close to the ground, and he was so enormous up there in the saddle, holding the reins, spurs shining through the stirrups. How could I confront a man on top of a horse?

Nevertheless, my life then often seemed to consist of the impossible task of confronting him, of defending myself and my mother from that man. Because she was afraid of him too. I knew she was, though she never said so. She became visibly nervous when he was due back home, hastily dropping whatever she was doing to make sure everything was in its proper place, the table set, the chairs neatly arranged and lunch ready to be served. She'd then rush to the mirror to comb her hair, brush imaginary flecks from her shoulders and smooth the skirt of her dress. Then she'd sit in the living room and wait. Waiting was another way of obeying him, of creating an empty space around herself for him to fill when he entered. And everything she said or did after that would be attentive and thorough, as if she were following an instruction manual to the letter.

She'd been a typist at a notary office on the same street as the barracks where my father worked. When he met her she was twenty-six years old, pretty and afraid. She'd taken the job because the salary was better than where she'd previously worked, but she felt oppressed in the notary's stuffy rooms. They were almost an extension of the barracks and there was a constant stream of uniformed men passing through, with their heavy footsteps and big boots and readiness to make fun of her or flirt—which she had to put up with in silence or else risk losing her job. She stuck strictly to her role as an employee, remaining calm and playing deaf, no matter how much they provoked her:

You married, love? Or are you hiding the ring to make out you're single? Look, she's gone red! She might look young, but I bet she's seen a thing or two. You know what they say, hicks make the best chicks. Laughter.

What would it take to get these papers processed sooner? Isn't there anything a nice lad like me could do to jump to the front of the queue?

Hunky, pal, a *hunky* lad, that's what you gotta say, or are you worried you'll frighten the girl?

So it was a surprise when one of these uniformed men began to appear with some regularity and the teasing stopped, miraculously, even when he wasn't there. And whenever he walked in, the others immediately saluted him, feet together, heels clicking.

She refused to believe that this man, who had fallen into the habit of popping in most days, and who the others respectfully called major, might be at all interested in her, insignificant creature that she considered herself to be. But she had to believe it when, a year and a half later, he took her to church and made it official. Naturally, this only happened after numerous conversations and a series of walks, for which she was dutifully accompanied by an older cousin (and, what's more, only after he'd conducted thorough research into where she'd been born and raised and found the results to be satisfactory, although she didn't find out about this until much later).

Here was a respectable, responsible man who didn't make fun of her, and who valued her qualities as a minor employee. And she was a respectable woman; humble, efficient, and modest. I think she saw marriage as a kind of promotion. Or salvation. She'd no longer have to worry about making her money last to the end of the month.

He lived in a small but comfortable apartment, with a fully-trained maid who would cook, wash, iron, and keep house instead of her (and who had come, she later found out, from his previous marriage)—reason enough to be grateful to the man who had given her this new life, a life she'd never even dreamed of. No one in her family had thought it possible, and so neither had she.

After all, she knew no one in Lisbon. She'd been born poor in the Alentejo and had lived with her godmother across the river from Lisbon in the small town of Montijo while training to be a typist. It wasn't easy to find a husband as a working woman of twenty-seven. People said nurses and teachers even had to get special authorization from their employers to marry. She'd never expected to have a family, but one year later I was born.

I think this was a relatively happy time for her, at least until I turned out to be a disappointment. Not to her—she liked me just the way I was, and tried her best to make up for my father's dissatisfaction. Which only made matters worse, because he thought one of the prime causes of my feebleness was the way she protected me from him. Disagreements began to arise and I felt responsible.

Then she withdrew into herself, finding refuge in small tasks that required silent concentration, while my father sat reading the newspaper, likewise in silence. She made lace doilies and embroidered placemats and tablecloths, until it became obvious we'd have to live life several times over if we were ever to use them all.

It occurred to her to sell her embroidery, but to my father this was unthinkable. The wife of an army major touting around her needlework—the very idea! My mother said nothing. Her hands now lay idle as she sat in the corner of the room, and my father found this concerning. After all, as everyone knew, the devil wouldn't let idle hands stay idle for long.

Something had to be done, he thought, before she started sitting at the window, sighing and paying too much attention to the passers-by (who always included plenty of men). Eventually, out of desperation, he decided she ought to learn the piano. This would keep her busy and improve their social status, since almost all the best families had a piano in the living room. He'd buy her one and arrange for a teacher to come to the house.

To his great surprise, my mother declined. Moreover, for the first time in her life she seemed to know exactly what she wanted: not piano lessons, but painting lessons. She'd always wanted to draw and paint and never had the chance, but now she'd like to learn.

Father agreed: piano or painting, it was all the same to him. In fact, when he thought about it he realized it would be a considerable advantage not to have to put up with the tiresome sound of a piano being played badly. Painting didn't make any noise, and as long as she didn't make a mess in the house and she kept all her paints and brushes in the attic, there was no reason why she shouldn't hire a teacher.

"Tomorrow morning, if you must," was his reply when she excitedly enquired as to when she might start.

And so it was that ten days later (the time it took for my mother to gather the relevant information and nervously present it to my father) Dona Auzenda entered our home. A new era had begun.

Suddenly, as if by magic, my mother's life was replete: she had a purpose. During the day she'd become so absorbed in her painting that she had to start using an alarm clock, setting it to go off shortly before my father got home. She'd then hastily tidy everything away, take off her smock and rush downstairs to check everything was in order, and be sitting in the living room on the stroke of midday, ready for my father to walk in. As if she'd been there all along and her heart wasn't pounding from her race down the stairs.

Over lunch, she made conversation—which meant agreeing with everything my father said, afraid even then of saying something wrong—and never once looked at the clock to check the time. But when she accompanied him to the door after coffee, the lost time seemed suddenly to make its presence felt: she'd glance at the grandfather clock by the front door and hurry back upstairs to the attic.

Dona Auzenda came twice a week. The two women seemed to understand one another, and I'd hear them chatting together and laughing. Dona Auzenda explained things, talked through different techniques, answered my mother's questions and gave demonstrations. But I don't think her being there was what mattered. My mother didn't paint for Dona Auzenda; she painted for herself, and discovered many things on her own. She often didn't ask Dona Auzenda's opinion and she certainly didn't show her everything she painted. My mother practiced, experimented, and discarded unsuccessful attempts as if she knew what she was aiming for right from the start. This was uncharted territory for her, and she was trying to move through it by following her instincts.

After a while, my father decided he might as well save the money and tell Dona Auzenda to stop coming. My mother continued to paint, for no one but herself.

I insisted on joining her as she explored this new world, and the times I spent in that attic were by far the happiest of my childhood.

I remember the house as a divided space: the dangerous territory of my father and the adventurous, secret world of my mother, with the stairs connecting one to the other. The attic was a limitless space; being there was like floating on air or sitting among the clouds. My mother would spread a piece of paper on the table before me and give me pencils, brushes, and paints.

Everything was possible. I only had to wish for something and it would appear: the sun, a bird, a tree, a blade of grass. That's right, she'd say, smiling. We were accomplices and we shared a magical power, each of us drawing away on our sheets of paper. We were the center of the world and the world obeyed us. We made the sun rise over the horizon, we put a car on the road, a windmill on the hill, people waving at the windows. Everything we wanted to happen, happened. Everything.

Art, I discovered, never ended. It was merely interrupted by tiresome and tedious tasks like eating, washing your hands, showering, going to bed, and sleeping. But it started all over again the next day as if it had never stopped. Every day brought something new, and the game of making pictures ran on.

The attic had a window from which we could see the river (we lived in an old building on Rua de São Marçal). It was really more of a skylight than a window, a glass rectangle in the sloping roof that could be opened partway. My mother was able to see through it from her chair, but I had to climb up on a bench. I never got bored of standing there and gazing out.

The river: a great stretch of water that changed color depending on the light. Boats moved between the two shores, small boats like yachts and tugs and the ferries that went back and forth, and big boats like the liners heading for the Atlantic. The river led to the sea, and the sea went on and on, and it was so big that you couldn't see anything else once you entered it. The sea was one of my oldest memories. It wasn't visible from the window but you knew it was there, because that's where the river was going.

Inside the attic was the river and inside the river was the sea. The river became the wall that wasn't there, that had been diluted or turned as transparent as the water itself. The attic had only three walls; the fourth was the river and the sea.

But there was a darker side to all this: sometimes when I woke up in the morning and ran up the stairs, I found the door shut. I'd bang on it with my fists and call out to my mother, as loudly and for as long as I needed to until she heard me. She'd eventually open up and give me a kiss, all smiles, but then she'd lead me back down the stairs and hand me over to Alberta, the maid, who would take me to the Botanical Gardens on Rua da Escola Politécnica.

I'd object, indignant, but she'd tempt me with the promise of sweets bought from the grocer's on the corner, which we'd pass on the way. Eventually I'd relent, still sulking, and Alberta would take me by the hand and lead me to the Botanical

Gardens, where I'd be made to play football with the other children.

I always escaped as soon as I could, however, and would tear back up to the attic, hammer on the door and call out again, with all the force I could muster. My mother would open the door, sigh and say I could stay, but only if I was quiet. She was finishing a piece of work and I mustn't disturb her. Otherwise Dona Auzenda would scold me.

With time I came to understand, vaguely, that I wasn't welcome in that world either. I came between her and her painting. And I wasn't see-through. She didn't need me in order to be happy up there, to escape the house through doors that opened up to her inside her paintings. To escape down the river, in the boats, to the sea she painted in blue. She was escaping me as well. I distracted her, getting in her way and demanding her attention when she wanted to be left alone to concentrate, to feel she was elsewhere. Was that it, then? Was I surplus to requirements, unwanted, the third wheel in an intense, passionate relationship?

That seemed impossible to me, and for a long time I couldn't accept that she didn't want me with her. But Alberta was always coming to get me from outside the attic door. I noticed she came evermore frequently, without even needing to be called; she'd just appear and lead me downstairs, where she tried to persuade me that my toys were just as much fun, the tin drum, the bugle, the wooden rocking horse.

The days would suddenly darken, there would be no more sunshine at the window. Until one day when I kicked my toys over and ran back up the stairs, Alberta in anxious pursuit. I barged through the half-open door to the attic and threw a bottle of paint thinner over my mother's work.

If she didn't like me, I didn't like her paintings. Or her. It was better to say it once and for all, and that's precisely what I'd done, without the need for words: I'd hurled the bottle against the wall, where it shattered into pieces, and I'd wailed as if the world had come to an end. Which, in a way, it had.

To my great surprise and, I imagine, the maid's even greater surprise, my mother hugged me and started to cry.

"You can go, Alberta," she finally said. And she let me settle down in front of a piece of paper for the rest of the day, and every day after that, until I started school and left her in peace again.

But that was over a year later and until then her space became mine, or at least that's how I understood it. Never again did I find the door closed and I was allowed to touch anything I liked. What I didn't realize was that she'd almost entirely stopped doing any work herself, and just watched over what I was doing.

Only years later did I find out, or rather did she tell me, that she'd sometimes work at night instead, once I'd gone to bed. But never for long, because my father didn't like her working when he was at home, which was understandable in a way because, after all, what had he married her for if not to have a bit of company?

I discovered the joys of cutting shapes out of paper and creating collages from magazines, of drawing pictures, of mixing flour and water into a paste to make papier-mâché models, of shaping objects and figures out of clay, which we'd leave to dry in the sun and then paint and glaze; we'd later bake them in a kiln, after Mother persuaded Father to buy her one.

Most of the time, though begrudgingly and not without loudly voicing his disapproval, he'd satisfy these requests of hers—her whims, as he called them. He agreed she should have something to amuse herself with while he was out, but was adamant that nothing must interfere with my education. We spent our lives running up against his vision of the world, which was in every way the opposite of our own.

When I proved a mediocre student at Liceu Camões in

every subject except art, when I started at the António Arroio art school, when I enrolled in the Lisbon School of Fine Arts, we went through long periods of open warfare at home, which got us nowhere and left us exhausted. My father repeated the same arguments time and again, with the pig-headed assurance and tenacity of the village know-it-all he'd never stopped being.

To him, people who did drawings and made puppets and clay figures like I did and sold them at fairs were no better than tramps or street performers. What they made today, they lost tomorrow; it was ill-gotten money, it might amuse them and others but it wouldn't last. And besides, you just had to look at the people who liked dolls, clay figures, and drawings: children, market traders, and lunatics. What respectable man had ever made a living from dolls?

If I wasn't cut out for the military, I could study to become an engineer, lawyer or doctor instead. Or an architect. Even a mechanic. Anything useful would be acceptable. But if I was going to spend my life making those useless things, I'd be nothing but a disgrace. An eccentric, unable to cope with the real world and normal society.

Not even when I got a distinction for painting or when one of my artworks won a prize did he show any sign of satisfaction or offer any support.

I was always a kind of catastrophe in his life, and although he eventually gave up trying to change me—catastrophes can't be fixed—he always found me difficult to accept.

The 25th April revolution changed nothing in our relationship, of course, but nor did it bring any surprises. We each carried on just as we had been; at the age of sixty-four, my father was as much a supporter of the regime as ever, and that wasn't about to change.

I attended rallies (gloriously, I thought, for the romance of the revolution was intoxicating), shouting out slogans and demands, and spent nights printing leaflets and sticking up posters, deliriously convinced we were going to change the world. I was eighteen, I felt euphoric and incredibly powerful. Because it was also a cultural and sexual revolution, freedom and joy in every sense. I fell passionately in love with several women, for the love of passion itself; eternal love, even if it only lasted a single day or night. I thought I'd never be faithful to just one woman. When all was said and done, what man could be? Women were everywhere, all around us, discovering the world just like us. Today was heady and life-affirming and all our tomorrows would be bright. We were eighteen and the world belonged to us. Our generation had been born dead but it was coming alive, out of the shadows and into the light.

I told you about these fleeting affairs because you asked me, and about the women in Berlin, tall, blond, intelligent, stunning. There were a few, of course—wasn't that always the way? If I had to pick one out, it would be Angelika, who was studying the cello (the Kunstchule also had a music department). I could have stayed with Angelika for longer but I didn't want to be tied down, I valued my freedom above all else and there was a whole world out there to explore. Besides, I knew I wouldn't be in Berlin for long; I wanted to spend a few years in the US, get to know other countries, see new horizons and continents. I loved Berlin, but I grew tired of the snow and the gray skies. I always knew I wouldn't be there forever.

I told you about these experiences and obliged whenever you wanted to know more. But I was always vague about my childhood.

"And your mother, what was her name?" you asked me.

"Luísa," I replied. "Luísa Vaz." Then I added:

"She always took my side, or was at least on the same side as me, though she never showed it. She almost preferred not to acknowledge the 25th April, to avoid engaging my father in a pointless argument. She just kept quiet, shut the attic door, and painted."

Painting, I thought later, was her way of escaping her limited, meaningless life. I hadn't ruined my parents' relationship: she'd become despondent long before I was born. Marriage wasn't the bliss it had promised to be; rather it was a dreary, narrow existence, with a hysterical man who was quick to anger and incapable of love. My mother never stopped feeling frightened and trapped.

But I didn't tell you any of this. I simply agreed when you said I must have inherited my creative side from my mother. That's why I signed my work using her name: Paulo Vaz and not Paulo Ramos. In her honor.

But there was no denying I'd also inherited a lot from my father, I'd add: I too had a bit of the village know-it-all in me, an old-fashioned side, with a bluntness and stubbornness that came from the soil. I had come to accept this about myself and I had learned to accept him too. I was his son, it made no difference that we'd let each other down. That was life; I had no regrets.

Especially because I'd had the last laugh, I told you. Just think, that prudent and sensible man who made sure his bank balance grew every single month started to play the stock markets in later life and lost everything. He came to see me with his head bowed, when I was back from Berlin for a fortnight in the summer of 1980. My mother had Alzheimer's, he told me, and could no longer manage in the house; she needed to go into a home and I'd have to pay for it. His pension wasn't enough to cover anything and he'd lost his savings on the stock exchange. I'd have to come to the family's rescue.

I felt the ground disappear from under my feet. I'd earned my money with the sweat of my brow, making countless sacrifices in the process, and I wanted to go back to Berlin. I suggested to my father that he sell the farmhouse in Beira, but he wouldn't hear of it and made one of his scenes. I realized I'd never convince him. He felt a visceral tie to the land there; the farmhouse and the estate were his roots, part of his identity, the very last thing he'd let go. He threatened to put my mother in an asylum if I didn't help. I caved in, ended up broke, and had to postpone my return to Berlin. That's when I went back to the Lisbon School of Fine Arts and took a job as a teaching assistant (on a teaching assistant's salary, although the work was more akin to that of an assistant lecturer). And that's how, a year and a half later, I met you.

But they were tough times at first. I was in a dreadful state, working like crazy, sometimes all through the night, because I'd found a gallery owner prepared to take a chance on me and I didn't want to disappoint him—or myself.

Luckily, I was able to live with Rui Pais for a year. He was always a good friend, Rui, he was finishing his Medicine studies and had an apartment all to himself, thanks to his rich and generous family.

"Forget about splitting the bills, pal. It's really no problem."

Rui was always like that, and it was a tremendous relief not to have to go back home and live with my father.

That was the version of events I gave you, Cecilia. Lying about just one detail, for the truth was slightly different and on the surface unbelievable: rather than playing the stock markets, my father had started going to the Estoril casino. I don't know whether it was before or after my mother got ill, although to be honest I think it was afterwards. He too was looking for an escape from life, his own secret world to sink into.

Everything had gone wrong, he was all alone and having a last roll of the dice. He cared little whether he won or lost. Nor did he care that he'd abandoned a mother with Alzheimer's to me, leaving me to support her by my own means. At least no more than he cared about deserting us and throwing away everything he thought was his, when really it was ours as well.

By the time of her death, towards the end of 1981, he'd drained all their bank accounts and savings. He owed ten months' rent on the apartment and had sold everything in it of any value (the landlord had been prepared to wait for payment out of respect for the major, who had used the extortionate cost of his wife's care home as an excuse).

Nor did I tell you that shortly after my mother went into the home, my father had dismissed Alberta. She rang me at Rui's apartment and said she urgently needed to see me.

She showed up looking the same as ever, her hair in a bun like my mother's, her clothes and shoes out of date and falling apart, also like my mother's.

I wanted to give her something to make up for her having been so coldly dismissed by my father after caring for my mother for so long, and indeed I assumed that was why she wanted to see me.

"God bless you," she said, taken aback. "But I've got my little nest egg, I don't need anything from you. In any case, I wasn't looking forward to putting up with your father without your mother around, you know what he's like, he made all our lives hell. My patience ran out, you can't imagine how it's been, you've only to look at him and he gets worked up. And now he's emptying the house, sending everything to Beira and saying he plans to go and live there."

She stopped for a moment and sighed, or rather took a deep breath, to summon the courage for what she was about to say.

"This was all a secret, you see," she began, speaking in a low voice as if she were in a confessional. "Nobody knew except me, but for many years, until she got sick, your mother sold her paintings. She gave me the money to look after, and here it is." She placed a plastic purse on the table, worn away at the edges.

"What are you talking about, Alberta?"

I didn't understand what she was saying.

She explained it again, her voice now almost a whisper, as if recounting a scandal someone might overhear from the other side of the door:

"She put her works up for sale in a stationer's shop, far enough away from the house that she thought your father would never go in. It was a small shop, on Rua de São Bento, the owner was a man named Senhor Correia. I took him whatever your mother sent, and called in from time to time to see whether anything had sold. They were mostly Christmas cards and wedding invitations at first, but they sold very well, and Senhor Correia even began to receive orders for other things. People wanted this or that painted, they'd say, done in such and such a way, and Senhor Correia would write everything down on a piece of paper and your mother would do as requested. Senhor Correia said she was very good and I thought so too; they were beautiful, the things she made, and you could tell she had a real knack for it.

"Later on, we started selling paintings too. I smuggled them out of the house in a shopping basket and Senhor Correia framed them and hung them on the wall, with little pieces of paper indicating the price of each one. They took much longer to sell than the greetings cards and invitations, but sell they did, one by one, and of course they were worth a lot more money. Senhor Correia subtracted the cost of the frames and took a little bit for himself, his commission he called it, and he wrote it all down on a piece of paper for your mother. She checked it over and said it all added up, that he was a very honest man and never tried to trick her.

"She asked me to look after the money and I hid it in the wardrobe in my room, inside this purse.

"You know what it was like. If your father had seen her with money he'd have taken it off her straightaway, because he always had to be in charge. And, of course, he'd never have let her sell her paintings. The world would have come tumbling down if he'd found out, Carmo and Trinidade churches and all.

"Keep it for me until I ask you for it, your mother said to me. And if I die, give it to my son.

"She hasn't died, but it's the same thing really, isn't it?" Alberta
said. "She won't be needing the money now so I'm giving it to
you, just like she asked me to."

She stopped talking and took a deep breath, as if a weight
had been lifted from her shoulders.

I took a few notes out of my wallet:

"Let me give you your commission too, Alberta. And thanks
for everything."

But she refused, almost offended.

"I can't accept that, it's the last thing I need. It was no trouble
at all, they weren't heavy, all I had to do was put them in the
shopping basket and Senhor Correia's wasn't so far away. I was
glad to help your mother. It was no bother to me and it was such
a balm to her."

After she left I went straight to the stationer's. Alberta had
told me the name of the shop, but couldn't remember the street
name. It was easy to find, though; there weren't many stationery
shops around there. I saw five still lifes hanging behind the
counter and before I'd even checked the signature I knew they
were hers. Senhor Correia took the paintings off the wall and
helped me to load them into the trunk of my car.

"That's an excellent purchase you've made, Sir, I assure you,"
he said, evidently pleased to have found a customer. "She was a
very good painter, you know. Most people have never heard of
her because she just signed her work LV and never appeared in
public, but she had her admirers. I've sold a lot of her paintings,
and a fair few Christmas cards and wedding invitations besides;
you wouldn't believe how many orders we used to take.

"I'm told she's died, or is at least in a very bad way, and you
know full well, Sir, that when a painter dies their work increases
in value. You won't regret buying these, that's for sure."

"Did she only paint still lifes?" I asked. "I mean, flowers,
fruit, objects . . ."

"It was mostly that," he said. "Or the sea. Beaches and the sea."

And with a slight nod of the head, he concluded:

"A very good day to you, Sir."

Still lifes. I hung those paintings on the wall and you often used to look at them, Cecilia. You often wanted to talk about them.

Like me, you went straight to the heart of them: the way everything was positioned, the arrangement as a whole, the dialogue between the different forms and materials, the light. The choice of flowers—roses, daffodils, toadflax, anthurium, petunias, hydrangeas, orchids—and how they complemented one another, the odd fallen petal, the shape and color of the vase, the surrounding objects. A glass bowl full of fruit, a couple of books, photos, an old candlestick holder.

No detail was left to chance, everything contributed, played its part in setting the scene and mood: vitality, order, serenity, concentration, intimacy. And solitude too; melancholy.

My mother had a natural feel for composition: everything was somehow more than itself, more than a simple flower or object. Yet the apparent harmony was tinged with disharmony. The fruit, for example, was somehow disquieting: red, fleshy strawberries and cherries, some of them sliced open, in a champagne flute; sensuality behind glass, always contained.

"She never studied art, she didn't know anything about it," I told you. "It was all instinct."

With the paintings in the trunk, I drove straight to my father's house. There would've been unfinished works in the attic—sketches, drafts, experiments, a whole back catalog I could take away with me.

But the attic was empty. My father had destroyed most of it, and thrown away all that remained. He'd dismissed Alberta and cleaned the entire house himself.

"Your mother's dabblings were worthless. They were just gathering dust."

I noticed that certain items of furniture and other objects were missing from the house: the grandfather clock at the front door, the blackwood cabinet, the dining room table and chairs, the two games tables and lamps from the living room. As well as all the silverware. But the only thing I cared about was my mother's work. I wasn't bothered about the rest and I didn't ask about it, partly because what Alberta had told me seemed entirely plausible: he was planning to move to Beira so he was sending everything there.

A bedside table where some photos of my mother used to sit was also missing. I asked my father about the photos and he said he'd put them in the desk drawer.

"I'll take them," I said.

"Go ahead. But leave the frames."

I ignored him and took them just as they were.

It was Alberta who alerted me to what was happening. On this occasion she didn't waste time coming to see me, she just called me on the phone. She sounded panicked.

"Your father's gone mad, he's gambling everything away at the casino. Go and see for yourself, he's running himself to ruin. Estrela next door told me, she'd been wondering why removal vans kept turning up outside and then her husband came across a load of things from the house for sale at the Feira da Ladra flea market. Your father goes off in a taxi every night—we all thought he had another woman, but yesterday Estrela's husband followed him in his car and it turns out he's been going to the casino. That's right, he saw it with his own eyes and that's the truth. Your father's ruining himself and he's ruining you."

It just didn't seem possible.

"Let's wait and see what happens, Alberta. But thanks for letting me know."

As I hung up, I realized she was in tears.

What if this unlikely scenario proved to be true?

My first thought was for the house in Beira. I rang the housekeeper: they'd been planting potatoes all week, everything was fine, yes, best wishes to the major.

So he hadn't sold that. At least not yet. For a moment I breathed a sigh of relief.

But that night I saw for myself that Alberta's story was true. I waited in a taxi outside my father's house, and followed him when he emerged and drove off.

He went all the way to the casino door. I went in after him and saw him hand over a wad of notes in exchange for his chips, seek out a table, watch for a few minutes, then join the game and become completely absorbed. So much so that when I went over to him and tugged him by the arm, he shrugged me off aggressively, showing no sign of recognizing me. He barely even looked at me, just brushed me aside like some interloper, his attention never really leaving the game.

I talked to Orlando that very night, at what must have been about two o'clock in the morning. Orlando was a lawyer and I knew he liked being in the office at that time, when no one else was there, with only low music and an overflowing ashtray for company.

"What can I do to get him banned?" I asked.

Orlando was used to crazy stories and nothing ever fazed him, unless it involved his friends.

He was quiet for a moment, then clearly decided it was best to be frank:

"You're screwed, pal," he said with a sigh. "We could try some kind of interim order, but a ban would take some time, you have to jump through hoops, gather witnesses, psychiatrists, the whole shebang. And what with the backlog of cases in the courts, by the time you got a hearing the house in Beira would've disappeared down the drain, because it belongs to your father and if he finds a buyer then even praying to Saint Anthony won't save you."

"But what if he goes through an estate agent and I get them to block the sale?" I asked, immediately realizing it was a stupid question.

"Can you see an estate agent passing up on a sale just like that?"

We both fell silent and sipped our whiskey. Orlando always kept a bottle in a cupboard. Then we talked some more, or rather he did, and I realized there was no quick fix to stop the world from coming tumbling down.

Horrible as it may sound, the heart attack that did for my father not long after that was the best thing that could have happened to me. If he'd lived much longer, the house in Beira would have been sold and I wouldn't have been able to handle the mounting expenses.

As it was, I sold the farmhouse and the estate, paid off my father's debts and was left with enough to keep my head above water for a few years at least.

No, I wasn't the least bit upset when he died. It was the best thing that could've happened.

I often wondered what my mother planned to do with the money Alberta hid for her. (When I opened the plastic purse I found a fairly measly sum, though enough to pay for three months at the home she was in.)

When she'd first started to save, years ago, what did she have in mind? Was it part of a plan of escape?

Did she dream of setting off one day, in search of a new life and a man who loved her? Impossible to say, though as a child I certainly dreamed of this on her behalf.

But how could she ever meet another man if she hardly

ever left the house and knew almost no one? If she wore old clothes and shoes, and cut her own hair then imprisoned it with clips? My mother and Alberta had the same hairstyle, the same hairclips, and their clothes were almost identical. I realized when I was young that my mother had to save every cent (although they were called centavos back then) because my father gave her only the bare minimum for her personal expenses. If she took me to a café, she'd order a cake for me but have a coffee and a piece of toast herself back at home, so as not to spend more than was absolutely necessary—the absolutely necessary being what she spent on me.

Her modest appearance and near-monastic lifestyle (monotonous, repetitive, and in a sense enclosed, with almost no personal resources) were part of my father's defensive strategy. The lower her profile, the more likely he was to keep her. Ideally, she'd only ever have left the house accompanied by him, and even then hardly at all.

That was his way of loving her, and he couldn't have imagined things being any different. He appreciated her presence at home, but rather as you might appreciate having an extra maid around, one more polished and refined than the first. But she was spared domestic duties, and ought to have been grateful for that.

If my father had been two or three ranks lower, if instead of a major he'd been an officer or a sergeant, or even a captain, she'd have had to combine the duties of wife and maid, taking care of all the household chores and getting nothing in return.

As it was, she was free of housework. Her role was to sleep with him, bear as many children as he and God so wished, join him at church or the cinema, play host on the rare occasions friends visited, make sure everything was tidy and keep him company over lunch and in the evening.

She performed this role satisfactorily and, in his eyes, there was no more to it than that.

But there was something else he demanded of her without even realizing: she (along with Alberta and myself) was to be the object of all his hysteria, frustration, insecurity, and irrational rage at the world. So addicted was he to shouting and causing a scene for no discernible reason that he didn't even notice he was being abusive. He imposed his authority so violently it ceased to be authoritative, it became a mere thundering voice, a storm unleashed upon us. All we could do was try to survive in the same ways wild animals do: by hiding, sheltering, fleeing. If we'd confronted him with the facts, he would've sworn blind that we were the hysterical ones; that society, the country, and the world were all hysterical and he was the sole innocent party.

Listening to him day in day out, I came to believe everything was my fault. If I could only be the perfect son, I'd tell myself irrationally, we'd be happy.

I think my mother must have told herself the same thing sometimes: that if she could only be perfect, we'd be happy. And we both tried to be perfect—until we realized he was impossible to please, and the problem lay with him rather than us.

Having tried and failed countless times, my mother was sure she couldn't change my father or the way he saw the world. But it seems it never occurred to her to leave, taking me with her and leaving him behind.

Her self-esteem was almost non-existent, and she felt incapable of dealing with the world on her own. She could've earned a living as a typist, as she'd done before. But how could she go back to typing after discovering painting? And how could she live off what she painted? She'd have had to earn enough to support me, too, because my father would've given us only the minimum he was obliged to by law. And she might've lost that battle anyway, meaning I'd have ended up with him. How could you hope to win a battle against an army major with a whole arsenal at his disposal? He'd have had us in his sights, with nowhere to run.

No, she could never have confronted him, however she'd gone about it. If she'd become a famous painter, he'd have seen it as a kind of theft or personal attack. And my mother doubted her ability and talent the same way she doubted her beauty, her strength, and her chances of ever being loved. So instead of standing up to him, she retreated, and she focused all her love on me because nobody could begrudge a mother's love for her son. Unconsciously, she withdrew more and more into herself, searching deep in her paintings for a way out.

Towards the end of my time in the house, I saw how she'd draw confined spaces, with narrow lines and uneven perspectives that seemed to converge upon a vanishing point. I didn't understand it at the time. It never occurred to me that she might go so deep into her painting that one day she'd enter the canvas, as if stepping into a mirror, escaping to a world where no one else could follow.

She did perhaps seem quieter than usual before I left Lisbon, more absorbed in her work and indifferent to what went on around her. She seemed to have no opinions or will of her own, but had anyone ever told her she had either?

However, the truth is I didn't really notice the change—perhaps because I didn't want to—and I went to Berlin.

She began forgetting the words for things and losing track of what she was saying, Alberta told me later. She looked at objects as if she'd never seen them before, with no idea what to call them or what they were for. She thought she was elsewhere, in a different time or place; she confused people's names, didn't recognize familiar faces. And then finally she forgot who she was, and couldn't remember her own name.

My father never contacted me when I was in Berlin, and I never wrote to him. I used to send my mother brief letters with news and receive drawings in return, in envelopes bearing Alberta's childish handwriting. At first I found this odd, but then I began to see it as our own special way of communicating. If my mother didn't write it was because she had nothing to say, her life went on as normal. To judge by the drawings—which these days were full of color and vigor—she was well.

When I saw her again after four years, the shock was hard to bear. I demanded to know why Alberta hadn't told me as soon as the illness began.

"I thought of writing to you hundreds of times," Alberta replied. "But what could I have said? What would you coming back to Lisbon have achieved? The doctor said there was no cure, and I decided it was best you didn't know. You'd suffer enough when you got back."

"And what about the drawings?" I wanted to know.

"She only did sketches by then, and at some point she stopped doing even them. But I found other drawings, ones she'd done a long time ago and kept in the attic."

When I visited my mother, that summer of 1980, she seemed to smile, not at all surprised to see me after all that time. One day she said the words "my son." Every now and then, albeit fleetingly, a fragment of her memory returned.

But then she'd start emptying cupboards or drawers as if she was looking for something.

"I'm tidying up," she'd say if anyone asked.

Or she'd take off all her clothes in the middle of the night and open the front door, completely naked and ready to make her escape.

The illness had installed itself and would advance relentlessly. She was fifty-two then, my father was sixty-eight and I was twenty-four.

The doctors called it Alzheimer's. But Alzheimer's is such a hollow name, a label for something we don't understand. The loss of mental faculties is different in every case, and so are the reasons behind it.

I sometimes think: she loved me so much that she gave up what she loved most because of me.

Artistic creation is difficult, and deeply selfish. To discover herself as an artist and follow that path, she'd have had to keep me shut out on the other side of the door. No matter how much I screamed and banged against it with my fists, she'd have had to have the courage not to open it.

It was all or nothing, there was no room for compromise. She either went down that path or she didn't. She couldn't just let me in occasionally, at certain hours of the day and for a limited time. She tried to set restrictions but it didn't work, I was always there and I got in the way. Her only hope was to take the attic to another house. But there was no other house. We both lived under the same roof and I needed her.

My father didn't spend any time with me. She never asked him to take me out so she could stay at home and paint, because she was afraid he'd be mean to me. And besides, he thought it presumptuous and self-indulgent that she took her work seriously. Painting was a hobby, something she was to drop the second he walked through the door and do only when her household duties were complete. And there were plenty of household duties to do, not least keeping him company and caring for their child. That's why he'd given her a child in the first place. And it was a mother's duty to look after that child, not dump him in his father's arms or leave him crying outside the attic door.

I know the guilt she felt towards me (and not the fear she had of her husband) was the hardest thing for her to bear.

Whenever she sent me off to the Botanical Gardens with Alberta and I didn't want to go, she'd continue her day with a heavy heart. She'd sit at her canvas and pick up her brush, but the morning would seem to have clouded over and the sun lost its shine. Her eyes would fix on a precise spot, she'd try to provide the right stroke of the brush, to apply the paint just so, but her mind would be elsewhere, her concentration gone, her vision shattered. Her hand, usually so firm, would feel tired, her wrist would refuse to comply. Eventually she'd stand up, go over to the window and gaze outside, but she'd see nothing.

Sometimes, very early in the morning, when my father had gone away for a few days and I was still asleep, she'd get up and rush into the kitchen, prepare a strong cup of coffee by way of breakfast and escape to the attic, dodging Alberta's torrent of trivialities:

We're running low on salt, flour, parsley and eggs, and the mint's run out. Would it be better to go to the market today instead of Wednesday?

Oh, and the iron's acting up. It needs taking to the electrician, I can't do without it, I've the major's shirts to iron.

It might even be best to go to the electrician's without telling the major, seeing as he's away, wouldn't madam agree?

The kitchen was a danger zone, best avoided. Then there was the vacuum cleaner, the telephone, the doorbell, the times Alberta would interrupt my mother with a message she thought was urgent but that could've easily waited. My mother's time became a series of fragments, which, after a certain point, it was impossible to piece together.

And the worst thing of all was my subdued face, red with tears, wondering why she wasn't there. I couldn't accept the shadows into which she retreated, the places she went to escape me. But escape she did. And I felt it: I knew I'd been abandoned. As if we'd been walking down a road together and she'd said: you sit down here in the shade, I'll be right back. And then disappeared.

Abandoned. Feeling that she didn't want me nearby. That she didn't want me at all. Because she didn't love me, because she sometimes didn't love me. But was it possible to love someone only from time to time? Surely you loved forever or not at all.

It was as if she'd taken me somewhere and then left. Promising to come back. But there was always that moment when she left, and losing her was like losing a vital part of my being. My hand, my foot, my tongue, my eyes. A part of me had been ripped off. At first I felt the same way about going to school, though I eventually got used to it because by some miracle the teacher understood me.

School saved us both, in a way. It meant I was looked after and she was free. Suddenly she had time to herself.

But my father did his best to poison that time, constantly interrupting it with his rants and complaints. My mother's life was a minefield. However softly she trod, however carefully she placed one foot in front of the other, with every step a bomb would explode and send her flying through the air in splinters.

I remember a dream I had: we went to Ramiro Leão so she could buy silk for a dress. We went up in a lavish lift and when we reached the top floor I noticed the stained glass panels all full of light above the stairs.

An eager assistant came straight over to attend to us, bringing out rolls of silk and unfurling them over the counter. Then my mother asked to see a different one: it had a beautiful, brightly-colored pattern and was soft to the touch, and would obviously have made a wonderful dress. I knew this was the one she'd choose, and was as happy as she was about having found it.

But when the assistant began to unroll the fabric across the counter, the silk, which had looked so glorious, turned out to be full of holes, as if it had been riddled with bullets. The whole roll had been spoilt. That's when I woke up.

But I didn't understand the dream until years later.

I visited my mother several times at the Hospital da Ordem Terceira on Rua Serpa Pinto. The old people's ward was—and I imagine still is—at the back of the hospital, on the second floor. It comprised a few yards of corridor with rooms on either side and a little dining room halfway along. The dining room only had space for four tables, but there were always empty seats because not many of the twenty-odd residents managed to eat their meals there.

At the end of the corridor there was a small lounge area with a cupboard on the wall and a clock that had stopped. A glass annex had been added and the TV in it was permanently switched on, though it was too hot to sit in there in summer, despite the air conditioning.

There was even a chapel on the ground floor, with some beautiful paintings that had presumably come from the original convent.

My mother hardly spoke, and she didn't know where she was. Sometimes she thought she was in our house in Beira or in Lisbon, and sometimes in an empty, unfamiliar place.

She could no longer walk and used a wheelchair instead, because she'd suffered a stroke since entering the home. She had her own room with a bathroom, an adjustable bed, an air mattress, a television, and a tiny balcony that overlooked the Chiado Museum café and allowed her a glimpse of the river.

In the summer, I'd wheel her out onto the balcony in the late afternoon. But she didn't see the lawn, the flowers, the parasols, the statues, the museum esplanade or the wisp of river in the background. She sometimes smiled vaguely, pointing out a sparrow or pigeon. Or a seagull, although there weren't many seagulls around there. She said very little and she didn't recognize me. If I showed her photos, magazines or postcards, she stared at them blankly as if she couldn't see.

She was clean and well looked-after, sitting there like a doll in her chair. Whenever I left, she'd wave goodbye over and over again. But she almost always ignored me while I was there, as if I were part of the furniture, ceiling or wall.

The wall, which was now her horizon. Like one of the many blank canvases she had sat facing, paintbrush in hand. Many lives ago.

They rang me one day at seven o'clock in the morning to tell me she'd just passed away. Was she feeling worse yesterday, did she have a bad night? I asked, but the answers were evasive.

I found out later that whenever someone dies during the night in hospitals or care homes, the rule is to let the family know in the morning but say it only just happened, and that there was no suffering. Like in the war, I thought, because that was more or less the formula they used when someone died in combat: it happened suddenly, the family would be told; he didn't feel any pain.

She was cremated in the Alto de São João cemetery, and I scattered her ashes in the river. So she could finally be free and head for the ocean. I liked to think of her like that afterwards, at one with the breaking waves.

But I told you all this in very vague terms, Cecília, and there were some things I didn't tell you at all. I was always ashamed of certain facts. And even more ashamed of my feelings.

CHAPTER II

Four Years With Cecília

WHEN I THINK back to that time between 1983 and late 1987, I think only of us, as if we'd lived those years all on our own.

But obviously there were other people too; our friends, not least Rui Pais and Teresa, Orlando, Jorge Reis and Matilde, Tiago and Marta, and Maria Rosa, who went out with Samuel and was also from Mozambique.

And there was the city around us too, of course. And the country.

I remember things in isolation. New Year's Eve (1983? '84?), for example, which we celebrated at Jorge Reis' house before heading home at five or six in the morning—or trying to, because the thick fog was getting worse and at some point we realized we couldn't go any further. We left the Vespa parked on the sidewalk somewhere and continued on foot, going round and round in circles, lost, until we came across a bar that was still open and we went inside to wait until the fog lifted and we could carry on back to Graça.

Disconnected memories. An unusually cold winter (the same one? A different one?) in which we installed a wood-burning stove in the studio, having realized that fitting a fireplace would've been more trouble than it was worth. That winter it snowed almost everywhere in Portugal, and even in Lisbon it froze over.

I don't have much of a head for dates, as you can see, but I can pinpoint half-a-dozen events thanks to the newspaper cuttings I kept.

In terms of the country as a whole, what I remember the most is the general state of crisis. By 1983, there had been ten general elections in the nine years following the revolution;

there were strikes, unpaid salaries, and mounting external debt. I remember they started knocking down the Monumental cinema and theater, despite all the protests and petitions we helped to gather.

Yes, I remember the theaters, the cinemas, the cafés. I remember us seeing Dreyer and Max Ophüls films at the Cinemateca, *Marianne attend le mariage* at the Cornucópia, *A Midsummer Night's Sex Comedy* by Woody Allen, and Bergman's *Fanny and Alexander.*

It was summer when we watched the Bergman film, the heat was unbearable and the country was on the verge of bankruptcy. Corruption was rife, companies were going bust and the extent of capital flight was alarming. The currency devalued, a new investment loan was requested and thirty tonnes of gold were sold. Compared to the rest of Europe and its immediate surrounds, our income per capita was higher only than Turkey's.

Two anti-corruption motions failed to get through the Assembly of the Republic due to the lack of a quorum.

Then taxes rose, there were more strikes, and the external debt grew by six hundred million dollars in six months.

The IMF intervened to prevent total disaster, but obviously did nothing to solve the country's structural problems.

After three consecutive years of drought, flooding caused by a major storm led to fatalities and thousands of ruined homes.

As 1984 drew to a close, a hundred thousand workers were awaiting overdue paychecks and many families went hungry. Yet only half of all our politicians declared their earnings.

The government promised to wipe out fraud and the High Authority Against Corruption was set up. New loans were requested to pay off old ones, our foreign debt rose again and there were four hundred and fifty thousand unemployed.

I remember us going to Aula Magna to see Carlos Paredes play guitar, and the sudden emergence of things like windsurfing, hang-gliding, and cordless telephones. I remember listening to Zeca Afonso, Zé Mário Branco, Sérgio Godinho, Carlos do Carmo, and when Maria João's first jazz record came out. I remember seeing *Apocalypse Now* at the Apolo 70, Visconti's *Senso* at Estúdio 222 in Saldanha—where we carried on our doomed fight to save what we could of the Monumental, even just the tower. But the tower was pulled down too.

There were the artists we admired, Julião Sarmento, João Cutileiro, Júlio Pomar, Cruzeiro Seixas, Eduardo Nery, Hogan, Menez, João Vieira, Paula Rego and countless others—and José Jorge Letria, and Adriano Correia de Oliveira, whose records we listened to. I think Adriano maybe died in 1982, and we lost others in those years too, Carlos Botelho, Mário Botas, Ary dos Santos, Alexandre O'Neill. I remember the books that left their mark on us, *Ballad* by Cardoso Pires and *Baltasar and Blimunda* by Saramago. And one novel in particular by Carlos de Oliveira, the name of which I forget, about a child obsessively drawing a house.

I remember the residents of Rua Norberto Araújo stopping us one day to tell us they paid rent to the Council but had no electricity, no running water, and rats the size of rabbits living in the stairways. I remember the thousands of people, most of them "returnees" from the former colonies, who the Council let live in abandoned buildings with no sanitation or even mattresses to sleep on. But for the most part, individual people and communities rallied round to try and help the half-million "returnees" get a roof over their heads and a new start in life. There was a sense of solidarity in a country where only seventy-five percent of the population had running water and electricity and salaries were the lowest in Europe.

Dissatisfaction with the legal system was widespread. It had ceased to function at all, and had a backlog of over a million cases.

A black hole appeared in the national finances of seventy-three billion escudos. Unemployment rose and income tax rates hit brutal levels.

The first Multibanco ATMs appeared. We watched *Paris, Texas* by Wim Wenders and *Rear Window* by Hitchcock. We saw Renoir and Buñuel films at the Cinemateca, I don't remember when exactly, as well as Fassbinder movies and *Andrei Rublev* by Tarkovsky, I think at the Quarteto. We saw Jorge Ben play at the Coliseu, and were in the audience for João Brites and O Bando.

We'd go to the beach in summer, on our own or with friends, drink in bars, dance in nightclubs, and in June, like everyone else, we celebrated the city's patron saints' days in Alfama.

Purchasing power collapsed still further in 1985, but Parliament voted to raise politicians' salaries by fifty percent.

The tax system was uneven and unjust, as usual. And, also as usual, after winter flooding, the summer brought forest fires.

In Lisbon, buildings collapsed like sandcastles. One of them with six families inside, on Costa de Castelo, because when the neighboring building had been demolished eighteen years earlier, no one had bothered to reinforce the supporting walls. A five-story building in Luís Bívar followed, then another in Praça do Chile.

We helped gather signatures for a petition (we managed to get 2,000 almost from one day to the next, and this without the internet, of course) to have the Martinho da Arcada declared a national historic landmark. Not only had Pessoa been a regular there, and written his *Message* there among other things, but it was also the oldest café in Lisbon. This the good people of Lisbon did manage to save.

At some point, I forget when, we saw *A Clockwork Orange* in the Quarteto. We went to an Opus Ensemble concert in Cascais and saw Maria João Pires at the Gulbenkian.

There were a handful of honest and respected politicians, it's true, and they made huge efforts to secure Portugal's future. But the country's fate hung in the balance.

There were always new hopes to latch onto: the possibility of joining the European Economic Community, for example, or the computerization of the tax system, which it was said would put an end to evasion and fraud. But no sooner had the system been computerized than the Constitutional Court denied journalists access to the list of politicians who had made income and property declarations.

Lisbon City Council couldn't even keep track of its own property portfolio and it was on the cusp of bankruptcy.

There was an outbreak of diphtheria in Bairro do Relógio. Tuberculosis still hadn't disappeared, and neither had child labor.

In 1985, Portugal joined the EEC, and in 1986, Mário Soares, for whom we'd campaigned, became President of the Republic and dominated the political scene.

1987 began with gale-force winds and snowfall on the coast, from Porto to Figueira da Foz. A building collapsed in Lisbon on Rua da Guia and another on Rua do Capelão, the latter having survived the earthquake but not sixty years of neglect. A third of all Lisbon residents were in unstable employment. Amália gave a concert in the Coliseu, which we went to, thinking it would be one of her last (though her powers were on the wane, she was still "the voice" of fado, and in fact her final show wasn't until 1994).

The Earth had five billion inhabitants and the Cold War was reaching its end.

In Portugal, the strikes continued. You took part in one at the School of Fine Arts in February, just before the death of the musician Zeca Afonso, protest singer of the revolution. Two groups of architects signed statements denouncing the Council for being autocratic and lacking a vision for the city.

In an interview, former presidential candidate Salgado Zenha accused all politicians in office of doing whatever they wanted with total impunity, a state of affairs that was incompatible with the rule of law.

The Lisbon stock exchange boomed and then, in October 1987, markets all over the world went into free-fall. People spoke of another 1929.

But these are just scattered recollections; the reality was far more complex. I find myself having to look back at my newspaper cuttings to piece together what happened.

Aside from anything else, our happiness in the midst of the crisis was something precious, a small miracle we guarded jealously from the chaos around.

We'd found balance in an unbalanced country, though we thought the bad times were temporary, transitional. Yes, great sacrifices had to be made. But after living through a revolution and its turbulent aftermath, we were prepared to pay a high price for a democratic, normal country.

But I don't want to talk about all this, Cecília. I want to talk about the life that was ours and ours alone.

Those four years are all a blur to me now, but I know we lived through them, one day at a time.

I remember an afternoon when Rui Pais leant us his car and we set off with a Brandenburg concerto in the tape deck. The sky's the limit, I thought as we sped along, the countryside flashing by outside the window. The sky's the limit.

It was as if I'd kidnapped you and we were on the run. Not from anything in particular; just for the pure thrill of being on the run together, racing faster and faster onwards.

But we weren't really on the run: nothing and nobody was after us. We weren't even fleeing the daily routine, since I had no such thing and you appreciated the shape yours gave to your days.

I wanted to be like you, a creature of timetables and routines. But I wasn't: I thrived on the unexpected, disorder and mess, tearing up the world I knew to see what surprises were revealed.

I liked to set off all of a sudden and with no plan, just see what we found. Dropping in on villages we had no idea existed, off the main roads and even the maps, talking to people, letting them tell us a bit of local history, which restaurant to eat in, where I'd find the best table, the best wine, the best bread, the best sheep's or goat's cheese, the best of everything they had. All for you.

Making love in chance hotels, opening the curtains in the morning and seeing a place we didn't know.

Sometimes I tried to adapt to your habits, to learn to organize my days and prevent the studio from descending into chaos. I was a terrible hoarder, forever accumulating materials and objects, allowing them to pile up everywhere in a big mess, then looking at them and feeling lost.

The studio was a huge space, with huge furniture—work tables, shelves, chests of drawers—a place where I was really the only thing that was small.

The studio shaped my life, especially once I stopped giving classes and focused on my work full-time.

I came across the place by chance after my mother died, on one of the little backstreets in Graça, having searched unsuccessfully for something in Castelo or Alfama. It was a former warehouse with high ceilings, a door that opened onto the street and a low window, which provided a glimpse of a patch of wasteland on the other side of a wall.

I immediately saw the potential of the place: the boarded-up window between the floor and the ceiling could be opened to create an extra area, a sort of mezzanine, and increase the capacity of the studio by almost a third.

That's how it began, with my rather megalomaniac vision. No space seemed too large for the projects I envisaged. I ended up living in the same building, renting a tiny apartment that had perhaps been intended for a concierge who never existed. It was convenient living so close to the studio, but the apartment was poky and the building didn't have a lift. Having almost too much space in the studio just about made up for the lack of space in the apartment, where no more than three people could fit at any one time. It was fine for one person to live in, two at a push. But at the time it was just me. A gallery was selling my paintings and I planned to spend a year in Lisbon, save some money and then head back to Berlin.

I never imagined you'd put up with it for long, because I wasn't planning on putting up with it for long myself. And it really was too small for more than one person.

But you got used to it with no trouble at all. You liked the apartment and the studio. I never told you that the studio sometimes felt hostile to me, that I felt myself under attack from the damp floor by the entrance, the peeling paint on the doors, and the rusty cremone bolt on one of the windows.

By moving around some of the furniture and other objects, we freed up some space on the ground floor, where there was good light from the window, and gave you your own workspace.

Your presence in the studio, from the late afternoon onwards and at weekends (because you still went to your classes), tempered the vastness of the space. You'd work by the window, I'd go up the wooden staircase and install myself beside another window on the mezzanine. Up there everything was smaller and snugger, and above all less chaotic. I couldn't see you from where I sat, but knowing you were there, working away by the window at the bottom of the stairs, protected me in a way from myself.

I concentrated on my work and appeared to forget about you. But your presence was enough to reassure me, like music in the background I could always hear. Even when you weren't there.

Sometimes I'd look down over the wooden bars of the mezzanine and see you standing at an easel, paintbrush in hand, or sitting drawing at one of the tables. You were concentrating too hard to notice me watching you.

I did various portraits of you, stealing a glimpse from the mezzanine railings from time to time. You rarely posed for me and I never posed for you, although you also did a few portraits of me. We didn't need one another to model; we had other ways of seeing each other.

They were relaxed, productive days, free from my usual anxieties. My fear of leaving work unfinished, of not finding a solution to a problem, of losing the unifying thread and suddenly finding myself lost in the darkness and the void. That was the other side of the creative fever that sometimes overcame me. When I'd lose track of time, unaware of hunger or tiredness, and stubbornly work on in a sort of euphoric or delirious fury. I wouldn't want to be interrupted at such times, and you understood this without me saying anything, as if we had a telepathic connection. You'd come and go with soft footsteps, nimble as a cat, and when you went off to bed and knew I'd spend most of the night down there, you'd leave a few slices of bread and a flask of coffee on the table.

You worked in a very different way to me. You assembled all your information patiently, making notes in tiny notebooks. The opposite of me, who jotted things down on random sheets of paper that I'd then lose; I never had notebooks, whereas yours went everywhere with you. You'd always find something worth holding on to, worth saving for later, in even the most improbable places.

You seemed to have no sense of urgency, often stopping in the middle of a piece of work and not picking it up again for a while. This didn't worry you; you never felt oppressed by the creative process. It was as if your abilities were endless and you had all the time in the world.

I, on the other hand, couldn't stand to be interrupted, and once I'd started work I expected everything I needed to come to me, without the chore of having to go looking for it. I was good enough to produce a piece of work quickly when an idea came to me—or insecure enough to need to. If I lost it then, it would be gone forever. There could be no medium-term, no possibility of postponing things, which was something you believed in and in a way even enjoyed—as well as your coursework, you had an array of projects that you'd barely planned or sketched out, and that afterwards you never turned into anything concrete. My time has yet to come, you possibly thought, endlessly gathering and assembling. But you knew it would come. Just as fruit ripens, just as the seasons change.

Or were you trying to live each day so fully that the next didn't matter?

As nimble as a cat. And silent. That's how your presence-absence was when you were in the house while I worked. You were inside me and around me. Soft as a fluffy toy, belonging to the space but not intruding upon it. You knew how to disappear, and you were so careful, so sensitive, that I trusted you completely. You'd never throw away one of my pieces of paper with a half-scribbled word or number, or a rubbed-out or crossed-through note. You moved among things, looking at them, interrogating them, but not interfering with them. And never breaking them. Like a cat jumping onto a table full of wine glasses and picking its way through them with millimetric precision, without disturbing a single one.

Sometimes you leant back in your chair in the studio and closed your eyes. With the early Saturday afternoon sun fanning out on the floor, or the moon rising outside the window.

And sometimes you'd close your eyes as you sat beside me, if we'd borrowed Rui's car and were driving long into the night. I could tell from your breath whether you were asleep. Sometimes I knew from the flicker of your eyelids that you must be dreaming, and I felt enormous tenderness towards you, sound asleep and defenseless.

And in the middle of all this was our love, exploding inside each of us, in our own bed or the others we slept in from time to time.

The chemistry between us, the almost magnetic attraction. We each had our own ways of being, feeling and thinking, but we stimulated and complemented one another. We were intellectual as well as physical lovers, I often thought. But the body has a wisdom all of its own and our bed was the most important place in the world. All lovers would say the same.

We knew we didn't need words to be happy, and we wanted to carry on that way.

Nevertheless, we established a few ground rules, like protective barriers laid out between us:

You had the same right to creativity as I did: we were equals. Whatever I did, it could never be at the expense of your own work or time. You said this, and I agreed. Indeed, I knew that if you had to choose between me and your own creative freedom, I'd be the one to go. If I ever got in your way. But I never did: as we both knew, I inspired you rather than held you back.

So we divided the chores in two. I think I probably even ended up going to the supermarket more often than you did, and that seemed normal to me, since after all I had more free time. I made dinner for both of us when appropriate, and even found that cooking every once in a while could be relaxing.

We normally ate sandwiches in the evenings, which is quite common in northern Europe but has yet to catch on in the south. We took turns cleaning the house.

We also decided (I came up with this one) that, except when we were collaborating on something together, we'd only show each other our work once it was finished. There would be no interference during the creative process.

This made sense to you as well. We regularly discussed what we were planning, and even gave each other suggestions at that stage. But once we'd got started, we worked alone. And when a piece of work was complete, the other person might talk about what they found most striking, and subjectively say what they liked or disliked, but there should be no evaluation of its overall quality, and no trivial words of encouragement, support, paternalism and the like. We lived and worked alongside one another, but we were entirely independent. Nevertheless, we communicated on a deep level, influencing each other in a positive way that we didn't fully understand. We didn't know whether this sort of relationship was common, whether things worked like this for other people, and nor did we care: it worked for us and that was what mattered. I wanted to protect us from disastrous situations I knew existed, or imagined existed, elsewhere.

For example, after seeing *Ma Femme Chamada Bicho* I remember agreeing with the widely held opinion that Arpad suffered from being too close to Viera, with her I-wouldn't-hurt-a-fly air. Madame wouldn't-hurt-a-fly Bicho used to visit her husband in the studio that he'd built in the garden precisely to get some peace from Madame.

Unlike me, he was rather docile; too docile to propose any rules, let alone impose them. He didn't dare send her on her way on the countless occasions when she'd open the door without knocking, asking "Je dérange?"—am I disturbing you?—only once she was already inside.

It was an effective strategy: she'd go away and leave him in peace for a while, until she thought enough time had passed for him to have produced something worthwhile, then appear at the door, all coy and curious, the admiring disciple come to visit the master.

"Je dérange?" she'd ask meekly, her voice full of sweetness.

And he'd relent, when he should have locked the door and shouted at the top of his voice:

"Oui, tu déranges!"

And so, thanks to his weakness, she was able to cast her

voracious eye around his studio, taking everything in within seconds, and then sweep out again having found the inspiration she needed.

A few days later, his ideas would appear, transformed, expanded, and metamorphosed into her own work. Forceful, substantial, as if they'd been her ideas all along.

So he threw out all the studies and sketches in which he'd been timidly trying to do something new, something she'd then developed and for which she received worldwide recognition.

I'm sure it wasn't always like that. It would be impossible to put up with for a whole lifetime. But it must have happened a lot.

Other people didn't realize what was going on because they were looking at the relationship from the outside, and Arpad's sweetness was disarming.

For Cesariny they were the perfect couple, Le Couple, the communion of two intertwined souls. Cesariny knew a lot about painting and poetry, and absolutely nothing about women.

The truly perfect pair, Le Couple, was us. Artists and lovers.

With Cesariny and Vieira-Arpad in mind, I painted a series of works about us, also called Le Couple. But we're not recognizable in them, obviously. We didn't need to shout our life from the rooftops nor scatter it on the wind. It was enough to experience it and be happy. Allowing one another space, protecting our individual freedoms.

I told you I didn't want children long before you ever even raised the issue. I warned you that none of my previous relationships had lasted, and later I said it wasn't possible to make art and raise a child at the same time. They were incompatible endeavors, each requiring exclusive dedication. I'd made my choice: I'd chosen my work. Besides, it was hard as it was earning enough money to commit to it full-time.

But eventually we realized you were here to stay. We never spoke of it, but it was clear from our day-to-day life together. I painted one picture after another, with an enthusiasm I'd never previously known. I was still in Lisbon, putting off my return to Berlin, and all because of a woman. I could stay here my whole life, I sometimes thought; I'd only want to leave if you wanted to as well.

You went on writing things down and making sketches. Attentive, focused.

But I knew you were preparing a work of some sort. You tidied the sketches and notebooks away into your chest of drawers—where they did not lie idle, for they were growing inside you, in the dark. They'd come out into the light in another form, when you opened the drawer once again to work on them.

But you postponed that moment. Not yet, you thought, sitting in the sunlight that fanned out across the studio floor. My time has yet to come. For now let's enjoy the wait, the space between one thing and the next.

Women love waiting, I sometimes thought when I looked down at you from the mezzanine without you realizing. You were smiling to yourself and seemed happy, putting a vase of flowers on one of the tables, or sitting in your chair by the window.

Perhaps, I thought much later, it was a secret daydream; one you never told me:

Wait here a moment, my little angel, I'll be back in no time.

I'll be back in two shakes of a lamb's tail, which means I'll be back before you know it.

It'll be like I was here all along. So don't cry, don't be afraid, don't miss me. I just have to pop over there and finish my masterpiece. And then I'll bring it back and show you how beautiful it is.

Please don't be sad, I won't be a second. It's just, there's something glowing over there, especially for me. I'll pick it up, that's all, like picking a flower. Then I'll give it to you. Your mother can fly, you see, she's a magical mother who does incredible things. I'll tell you all about them one day.

I don't want to leave you, but any second now that glowing thing will pop like a bubble and vanish into thin air.

Don't cry, please. Please don't need me right now, don't call out when you don't see me. Don't force me to choose between you and the other thing, because if you do, you won't like what I choose. If I don't go and get it, I'll die. Then you won't have a mother at all. So don't cry. Let me go. I promise I'll come straight back.

I promise I'll come straight back, but I end up further and further away. I've slipped into a dream and I want to dream it through until the end.

Yes, of course I think of you, I feel your weight in my arms, but my body has become so light I feel I might fly if I flapped my arms. Spaces open up with every movement I make and new things appear, things I couldn't see before.

I can hear music inside my body and all around me, and it takes me along with it. There's something glowing that belongs to me, but it seems to retreat as I approach, it blinds me and fascinates me, because I can't seem to see beyond its glow, but I know that it exists only fleetingly and that it will disappear if I don't get there in time, that it will be within my reach only for a moment and that I'll die if I don't manage to grasp hold of it—

You didn't know it was a trap. That the glowing, fleeting thing you saw was not a miracle but a curse.

You hadn't yet learnt that works of art are egocentric, all-consuming, and demanding, that they're the product of pure, hardened selfishness, that they're born of the fine line between success and failure.

And nor did I tell you. You'd work it out for yourself in due course, and then live your life stuck between heaven and hell. As I did.

Or did you know already, and was that why you put things off? Was the real reason you never started working on anything that you knew it would be a treacherous path, and that you couldn't stop once you'd begun? Were you preparing as thoroughly as possible on land, summoning the strength to untie your moorings and launch into the sea?

Anticipation was something to savor: everything in suspense and full of promise.

Perhaps, I thought much later, you had this dream and never told me: the dream of having everything in life, your work *and* a child.

But your feet were planted firmly on the ground and you took the pill. That was the greatest of discoveries, truly liberating, the end of fear, I thought numerous times as I made love to you. Even more important than sending a man to the moon.

Four years is no time. And, viewed from a distance, our four years together seem a rather homogenous period—consistently happy, but every day more or less the same.

However, that isn't entirely accurate. One day, in our third year together, something different happened. I was on the mezzanine, so engrossed in my work that I didn't notice anything.

It was only when I went down the staircase hours later that I realized something had changed: on your lap, wrapped up in a cloth, was a very tiny cat.

You smiled and put your finger to your lips, to indicate I

wasn't to speak. And in a very soft voice, so as not to wake the sleeping cat, you told me you'd found it under the window ledge, making a sad, strangled meowing sound.

You'd gone outside to get it, and it hadn't resisted at all when you picked it up. You brought it inside, gave it some milk and wrapped it in a cloth. And now there it was, asleep in your lap, and you seemed very pleased about the whole thing.

"Great. Now put it back outside where you found it," I replied, antagonistically. "Its family must be looking everywhere for it."

But you weren't convinced. It was a tiny abandoned kitten and it couldn't survive on its own. Besides, you didn't have the heart to put it back outside, all hungry and cold, after having opened the door to it.

I could tell that as far as you were concerned, its family was us now. It had become part of the household.

I shrugged my shoulders wearily. Forget about it for now, I thought. It won't be here long.

There was no way I'd ever tolerate living with a cat, but I wasn't prepared to argue about it right then. So I just said, rather brusquely:

"I'm going to have a shower then let's eat."

You called the cat Leopoldo. He was ginger and white, a stray cat from the Lisbon rooftops. Just like all the others you see out in the streets, sitting hungry in gutters, running away from dogs, hiding under cars.

The only thing I hated more than stray cats was house cats. Beloved of little old ladies with no other company, house cats would sit cozily on low-lying window sills and press themselves up against the glass, all warm and snug inside, to look out with disdain at people walking by in the rain—to look out mockingly at me, hunched up in my raincoat, my collar raised in ineffectual defense, because as ever I'd left my umbrella somewhere.

I hated Leopoldo, it's true, and I did everything in my power to make him disappear. I left the doors and windows of the studio open, and I even used to put him on the sidewalk outside and close the door when you went out, Cecilia. But he always came back, meowing beneath the window like on that first day, waiting under the ledge where you'd found him. And I'd have to go back outside and bring him in, so you wouldn't know what I'd been trying to do.

My plan was somehow to make him leave for good and then present you with his departure as a done deal, as if it had all happened by chance:

"He must have found a window open and jumped out. Not surprising, really, now the weather's improved. It's spring, it's stopped raining. He was a stray cat, after all."

But I didn't know how I could get rid of him without using violence.

In desperation, I suggested you offer him up for adoption via the Society for the Protection of Animals. The idea fell on deaf ears.

I phoned them myself the next day anyway, while you were out. They already had too many animals and too few people to adopt them, they said, and couldn't accept any more for now.

I tried the Association for the Protection of Stray Animals, which seemed a much more appropriate place to me anyway, for he was still very much a stray. Just because he'd strayed into our lives by chance one day it didn't mean he could get settled here. We were a fully established community without him and we weren't accepting new members. We hadn't announced an opening or advertised for candidates. He'd intruded, plain and simple. He had to accept this and be on his way, fulfilling his destiny as a stray animal.

But the stray animal clearly had no intention of straying any further. On the contrary, he made himself well and truly at home. And he assumed as his what was by rights ours. He shamelessly occupied the best position on the sofa, curled up on my chair or yours, took up prime position on the rug in the alcove in the afternoon, when the sun shone in.

Thus he occupied not just the studio, but the apartment too, taking possession of all the places he considered most comfortable, according to the time of day and the height of the sun.

In the morning, his favorite place was our bed, still warm from your body and mine; to my outrage and indignation, I found him several times hidden among the folds of the duvet, beneath or on top of which we'd just made love. I chased him away furiously with the first shoe I found.

"Blasted cat," I'd fume, just as I did whenever I had to tip him onto the floor after coming across him snoozing in my chair. As if he owned the place, as if the owners of the place were not in fact us.

Eventually I openly argued with you.

If you insisted on having a pet, I said, at least let it be a dog. I went on to list all the arguments in my favor, that is to say, in favor of dogs:

A dog is a friend who's forever ready to offer and receive affection. A dog would come running to greet us when we came home, jumping around in excitement. It would be equally happy to go for a walk or stay at home; it would agree to our plans, barking for joy, whatever they happened to be. A dog gives and returns love, and indeed it gives much more than it gets. There's no better friend in the world, as plenty of books say. Including *The Odyssey*. When Ulysses returns home, he finds only the old, decrepit dog, laid out on a pile of manure, waiting for him to arrive so it can die. Because that's what dogs are like: they sacrifice themselves wholeheartedly.

Let's get rid of Leopoldo and buy a dog.

What was more, now that I thought about it, I'd always wanted a dog. I could name it Argos, like Ulysses' dog.

But you wouldn't budge an inch. It wasn't your fault I'd never had a dog. If it was so important to me, how come I'd never mentioned it before? Why hadn't I rushed out and bought one before Leopoldo came along? The word "dog" had never once come out of my mouth, and most likely never even entered my head. I'd only thought of it now because I didn't like Leopoldo. I didn't seem to understand you couldn't just send him away, not after having allowed him into the house. He was a friend, in his way, and you couldn't treat a friend like that. I had to stop blaming him for everything I could think of. Especially the heinous crime of not being a dog.

I must have complained about him to you a million times. Then one day, lying on the bed in the place where I'd normally find him curled up, there was a letter to me signed "Leopoldo."

It was his turn to complain about me: he was indignant at how unfairly I treated him, constantly accusing him of everything and nothing. And he had never opened his mouth to speak badly of me. Not once.

He was quite sure I'd never heard him say Paulo Vaz sat in my chair, Paulo Vaz jumped onto my bed, Paulo Vaz walked over my newspaper; Paulo Vaz left hairs on my duvet, my pillow, my rug.

No, he continued, he'd never complained about me. Furthermore, he referred to me by name, Paulo Vaz. He didn't say "the man," whereas I wouldn't even deign to recognize that he had a name, let alone use it, always arrogantly calling him "the cat" instead. Which he disliked and indeed felt offended by, because "the cat" was the general term and he was unique, different from all other cats, which was why he had a name: Leopoldo. He was an individual, with his own personality, just like me, and he had the same rights.

It was tremendously insensitive on my part to refuse to recognize him as an individual, instead confusing him with an entire species by calling him simply "the cat."

I never expected this witty, ridiculous letter you'd written as a joke to change my relationship, such as it was, with the creature, though from then on I did occasionally and ironically call him Leopoldo.

However, looking back I wonder if I started paying more attention to him after that, seeing our intruder properly for the first time.

I realized why you'd given him the unlikely, almost imperial name of Leopoldo, which you sometimes shortened to Leo. He had a lion in his name. And he was the same color as a lion.

I remembered the little lion cub you'd been given as a child and then had to let go: you'd got him back, in a roundabout way. Admittedly he'd been downgraded to a cat, but that seemed good enough for you under the circumstances. A little pet lion, which unlike the other one would never grow too big or be taken away.

And which, despite appearances to the contrary, had retained his wild side. He pretended to adjust to us, but the jungle shone in his green eyes, in the tips of the claws he used to scratch the chairs and curtains, and in the ferocious way he turned to face me one day, growling, after I'd swatted him away with particular vehemence.

I began to observe him as he slept the afternoon away on the windowsill or alcove floor, stretched out to the full, legs splayed, the sunlight landing square on his belly.

He had a triangular scar by his mouth and one tooth that stuck out, vaguely suggesting a bat or vampire. As I listened to his rhythmical purring, it was as if I'd sneaked into an old lady's bedroom as she slept, the poking-out tooth seeming strangely like a glimpsed undergarment.

I suddenly found myself drawing cats, making sketch after

sketch, looking at them in new ways and surprising even myself.

The cat and I spent most of the day alone together, in the studio or the apartment, and I had plenty of time to use him as a simulation or model. He might be good for something after all, I thought, staring at him. That is, good for more than just graciously allowing you to make a fuss of him when he jumped onto your lap in the evening.

Until then, I thought that was the only thing you got in return for the hundreds of tins of food he demanded, the dozens of sacks of cat litter he forced us to drag through the supermarket aisles so we could change his litter tray before it started stinking too much. Because Leopoldo was far too imperial to relieve himself in the street.

"Only dogs do that—you can't take a cat outside to pee," you'd say, maybe worrying he'd run away or be hit by a car.

He was certainly a relatively clean creature. He used to make a little hole for his excrement and then attempt to bury it afterwards, though he'd always misjudge his strength and kick litter all over the floor. He also had the habit of urinating outside the tray, probably to mark his territory, and we'd have to mop it up with floor cleaner or bleach.

It goes without saying that I always left these tasks to you, since you were the one who wanted to keep him. And so you became his maid, his servant, and in exchange he allowed you to stroke him in the evenings as you sat in the corner of the sofa.

But since becoming my model, he served more of a purpose. Now it was my turn to use him without his knowledge: I could exploit him, make him pose for me for free, twenty-four hours a day if I wanted to, and he didn't have a clue.

I began to study him more closely. I learned what made him tick, and discovered his routines and hiding places, even the most secret ones: in drawers and wardrobes; and underneath benches, chairs and the kitchen table. Once I found him dozing on a sheepskin rug, perhaps because in a way it resembled him, at least more than anything else in the house.

I caught him smelling, with some curiosity and no little delight, a plant you'd put in a vase on top of the washing machine. He circled it, sniffing it, sinking his whiskers among the leaves and then lying down beneath them as if they were trees.

The cat's pleasure in discovering the plant, the plant as the cat's alter ego, or as a modified animal itself. The plant in the cat's dreams: a mysterious being from another planet, vegetal, but also needing to feed itself, also breathing and growing.

I saw him contemplating the sprouting of new leaves, the appearance of a bud, the bud opening into a flower: the cat's fascination with the flower, his trembling mouth and whiskers.

The plant as a messenger from another world, a world the cat didn't know existed, though he sensed, somehow, that there was life beyond his own universe; beyond the walls of the house, the corridor, the front door and windows. There was something else out there, something unimaginable he could only guess at.

Leopoldo at the window. His insignificant profile, head cut in two by the door, allowing just one eye to be seen.

His anxious whiskers, always in motion. His life as a semi-prisoner, spying on his surroundings from his post on the windowsill, sniffing the clean air beyond the open window and suspecting that the winged creatures that called out sharply in the late afternoon sun, and which he followed with astonished eyes until they flew out of sight—suspecting that these mercurial, unnerving beings were deliciously edible.

He knew this for sure in his dreams and it made him anxious—he knew many things, but only in dreams. For example, cruelty in its purest form: this was something he held deep inside himself, something he'd never unlearned. He could sink his teeth into the tender flesh of a bird, hold it firm in his mouth, contemplate it, trembling, until a death-rattle in the bird's chest or neck area told him his teeth and claws had won the fight. Then he'd lay the bird gently on the ground and pull out its feathers with his paws, the better to bite into the naked, paler but still living body in its coating of soft, greasy skin.

He knew about these things, and many others, without ever having experienced them.

That's why they troubled him, made him jump off the windowsill and pace around nervously in the few feet of concrete outside. The stretch of concrete was bounded by a wall that was too high for him to scale, especially since there was no room to build up any momentum.

He evaluated this situation rigorously, walking back and forth between the house and the wall. It was always too high. And even higher up was the sky—and the sun, a giant eye, watching his every move.

At night, mostly in summer but also in winter, he'd see a bright, luminous thing that grew larger and fuller. Sometimes it floated high above the wall and sometimes it seemed to balance right on top of it, a shiny white ball, complete and strangely defiant.

Whenever there was a full moon he'd stand in the little concrete corridor between the studio and the wall, waiting for something to happen. He had no idea what that something might be, only that there was a possibility of it happening. Even during the daytime. The warmth of the sun, for example, always came as a surprise to him, even though it was there every day. And then there was the wind, which brought him all manner of smells. He could spend all morning trying to decipher them, especially the ones he didn't know.

As if that wasn't enough, all of a sudden, in those few square feet of cement warmed by the sun, a lizard might appear. If he was alert and quick, and especially if he managed to sense it before seeing it, he might be able to pounce at the precise moment the lizard made for a crack in the wall and be rewarded with a piece of its tail, a still living thing that he'd then clutch between his paws.

Little day-to-day revelations: the world unveiling itself before the cat's fascinated eyes.

And the frustration of domestic cats, urbanites raised in apartments with no outside space; neurotic cats, prisoners, chasing their own tails.

Cats that fall from fifth-floor windows (inadvertently, their owners think; the cat must have dozed off and lost its balance, it was an accident. They never stop to wonder whether maybe their cat couldn't take it anymore and jumped). Cats from other neighborhoods, and especially cats from bygone times when people lived in little one-story houses where doors were left ajar and windows were conveniently low down; where walls were easy to jump over, neighbors were friendly and everyone had a proper backyard.

Leopoldo's trials and tribulations, and the magic formulas he invents to make the universe yield to his wishes. Whenever you went out, for example, he'd take your place. Sitting in your chair was his way of denying your absence, filling it with his body. To oblige you to return, he occupied your space.

It was even possible that a tiny part of him loved us. That's why he jumped onto your lap at night, looking for cuddles. Your hand ran over his fur like a giant, reassuring tongue. He went to you seeking pleasure, and licked your hands and face to give you pleasure in return. Animals lick to give and receive pleasure. As do humans.

Poised motionless on the windowsill as if untouched by time, looking out at the world though the narrow slits in his half-closed eyes. Partially with us and partially elsewhere, in a place he didn't talk to us about, because he shielded his private life from us, keeping secrets and hiding his feelings. Did he fear his opening up to us would be rebuffed?

He always seemed cold and indifferent towards us. At first I thought all he cared about was the house and his place in it, and we were mere servants to his comfort. It worried him when he didn't have enough water, milk, food or fresh cat litter, and he'd make any concerns he had clear by brushing up against our legs. Other than that, we might as well have not been there. With time, however, I came to see that wasn't entirely true. He did have a relationship with us, despite the untamed side to his nature, which he'd managed to hold onto despite several millennia of human dependence.

I very much shared this side with him. It made it easy for me to understand him, to follow or even pursue him, in the ferocious way I had of working. I had to look at him from all angles, pay him insatiable attention, get inside him somehow and see the world through the slits of his eyes.

Then I trained my eye on the studio and the apartment, which had become central elements in my painting for the first time. I'd always been drawn to travel, the world and wide-open spaces, but here I was discovering new secrets, intimate and enclosed. Leopoldo made me realize it's what's inside things that counts.

And I drew you and painted you, finally painted you, in this context. With the cat; part of the cat's world.

I sold all my cat artworks very quickly, except the few I decided to keep because I thought they might represent an important moment in my artistic development. Something told me they could turn out to be relevant one day.

In one of them, you're sitting in a low chair, knitting, with the cat curled up asleep beside you in a basket. The chair and the basket are floating in a sort of intergalactic abyss, which the woman and cat are part of as well. The woman is listening to the soft purring of the cat. She'll never finish her knitting. They're alone, but deeply content in the immensity of the moment, the cosmic void.

It's a snapshot of pure existence, pure unconsciousness, wrapped in the folds of time. The woman wants nothing more than the silence that enables her to carry on listening to the cat's soft purring, and the cat wants nothing more than to be lulled to sleep by the light jingling of the woman's needles, the almost imperceptible sound of unraveling thread. They're both linked for an instant that never ends, as if inside a time capsule, untouched by the vast empty space around them.

Another painting: the boredom of life on a rug, life behind glass. The cat mocked by the windows, mocked for not daring to go through them. Sensing that he could, if he wanted to, pass through walls, turn himself into a lion or a tiger, or an evil cat, a bewitched cat flying on a broomstick. But resigned to staying put, to being merely decorative and taking his place among the other household items. Pretending to be daydreaming, but really reflecting on his situation and gazing out through the window. Weighing up the pros and cons of staying. Because despite everything, he has an open window before him.

He hesitates, all of a sudden unsure where he belongs: in the great outdoors of sloping rooftops and rain, or inside a wardrobe or in any of his other favorite domestic hiding places?

I focused on the moment when he wavered, lost: caught between the jump, which has started to form in his tensed back legs, and the failure to jump, which becomes the act of nonchalantly licking saliva onto one paw, propped up like a kangaroo, with the other paw in the air looking somehow too short.

These works from the series *The Cat* and *Cecília and the Cat* (or so I later named them) sold for quite a lot more than expected, especially considering they were no more than a half-dozen weeks of intensive work.

Maybe Leopoldo wasn't entirely useless after all. I even grew accustomed to him being around, having spent so much time staring at him. So it came as a bit of a shock to me when I heard you calmly declare one day:

"The vet says it's time to castrate him."

"Time to what?" I cried, as if I hadn't heard.

"To castrate him," you sighed. "But I can't bear to think of it."

I looked into the matter, which was something I'd never considered before. Everyone I spoke to said there was no way round it: this business of pets mating through adverts in newspapers was only for pedigree cats and dogs; Leopoldo was of no particular breed and nobody would want him having anything to do with their precious felines. His only hope was alley cats, but he couldn't be let loose in the traffic to go in search of a girlfriend. Nor could he just be left as he was, because tomcats who hadn't been snipped became desperate in January; they climbed the walls, constantly excited, covering rugs, armchairs, cushions, and sheets with their sperm. When it was all over, there'd be a strange smell in the apartment that would never leave.

"Yet another reason for us to get rid of him," I said irritably when you got home that night. "This cat has brought nothing but trouble."

"He's brought other things too," you said, unflappable. "Including money."

"As if the cat were the one with the talent," I exploded.

You ignored that comment, and that was the end of the conversation.

When you went to class the next day, I picked Leopoldo up and carried him out into the street.

"Off you go," I said. "Go and get frisky while you still can."

He sat on the curb and didn't move.

"Mate, they want to give you the snip. Don't be daft, make a run for it."

It was a friendly piece of advice, spoken man to man.

But instead of taking off he ran back to the front door and into the studio. I picked him up again ready to put him back out in the street, but he started wriggling his head, flexing his claws and hissing. He was ready to bite and scratch me if I persisted.

So I let him go and he ran ahead of me, back into the studio.

The last time he'd truly be a cat, I thought.

You took him to the vet the next day, and when you got back you looked almost as exhausted as he did.

"He hates going in the carrier basket," you said. "He was tying himself up in knots trying to force open the catch. He won't even put up with it for a few seconds."

I didn't want to know. You needed to unburden yourself, but I wouldn't let you.

"Spare me the sob story," I snapped. "The cat's yours after all."

"Well, nothing happened in the end," you said calmly. "I took him to the vet, but then I just brought him home again. I couldn't bring myself to have him snipped.

"When the time comes, he can go out prowling the streets," you added, much to my alarm. "I'd rather he get hit by a car than have to stop being himself. We'll need to start opening the door for him when he wants to go out, that's all."

It was partly thanks to the *Cecília and the Cat* and *The Cat* series selling so well that I decided to take a chance on buying the studio. The owner didn't want much and he let me pay in installments. I still had a decent sum left over from my inheritance, and Rui assured me it was a good deal—we could always rent it out, or do it up a bit and sell it on.

The night I signed the contract, we went to a fado concert with Rui and Teresa, Tiago, Mariana, and Orlando.

I remember your course was coming to an end, and you were beginning to leave your classwork to one side and do your own thing. You chose Lisbon's patron saints as your subject, and already had plenty of sketches: you imagined them escaping from the churches and sticking two fingers up at their vestments, silver incense-burners, golden candlestick holders, glass cruets, jade and jeweled chapels; they jumped down from their altars and ran out into the street. They fled the papal court and the patriarchate; turned their back on the sumptuous, intimidating theater of Rome and the self-important Cardinal; shunned the solemn words and extravagant gestures of the pulpit, the resounding sermons, the smell of burning candles, dead people and the sacristy; they broke free from all this and burst out into the streets to dance.

All around them people stared, open-mouthed, at what they had always known but never dared to believe: the saints are made of flesh and blood, just like us. Your sketches told the whole story in half a dozen frames: the saints had grown tired of posing mute and motionless on their altars, and so their joints became flexible, their wooden heads, legs, and arms started to move and they adopted different positions and poses. They began to change their clothes too, dressing for the occasion. That was their first act of daring, but they did it surreptitiously, pretending they hadn't meant to. Then they went out and joined the street theater in Pátio das Comédias, in amongst the actors and puppets. They attended street parties, in disguise at first, but then openly joining in, taking people by the hand, spinning them round, part of the throng, and soon a party wasn't a party unless they were present.

And there they are, in the working-class neighborhoods of Lisbon for the June festivals, knocking back wine, scoffing sardines, and dancing, just like everyone else.

Saint George danced with the princess he'd saved from the dragon, and then, when the princess went to dance with someone else, he danced with the dragon, though it had lost its head and tail somewhere along the way; Saint John danced with a nun who'd thrown away her shoes, coif and veil; Saint Peter danced with a bride, rosy-cheeked and tubby, perhaps his own bride-to-be, for she laughed a lot with him; Saint Anthony had just enlisted and was dressed in a soldier's uniform, and he went to dance with the maid, who he had helped climb down from a ladder leaning against a window; and Saint Roch danced with his dog.

I looked at the sketches and laughed along with you, then I gave you a hug. You'd made a flying start and nothing could stop you now. The course didn't matter anymore, or the School of Fine Arts or any other college, for there was a whole world out there.

There was a whole world out there and it belonged to us. The magic recipe was talent and hard work; talent we had in abundance, and hard work depended on our effort and will. We'd get there. It was just a matter of jumping on the Vespa and taking off.

And then there was the day when you climbed the steps to the mezzanine to talk to me. You didn't look at the picture I was working on or even come towards me. You just said:

"When you're next able to take a break, I need to talk to you."

I could tell something was wrong because you didn't move from the top of the stairs. So I stopped what I was doing and went over.

"Hug me," you said, hugging me first. "Hug me very tight."

When I did, you smiled, and I was relieved. You'd seemed so solemn and unsure of yourself that for a second I'd been expecting bad news. Your parents, I thought—perhaps one of your parents had fallen ill or died.

But now you seemed happy, nestled up close to me with your eyes closed. All was well, then, you'd just wanted a little affection after some minor setback in your day.

I kissed your eyelids and waited for you to speak. When you opened your eyes you looked deep into mine.

You were silent for a moment or two and then said you were pregnant. I let out a guffaw, thinking it was a joke, though one in slightly poor taste. The pill offered strong protection and I'd always been sure we were safe.

"I stopped taking it," you said, as if reading my thoughts. "A few months ago."

I couldn't believe what I was hearing. And when you didn't say anything else I got angry, failing to find the right words among the many racing through my head.

I don't know how long it lasted. I don't even really know what I said, what I shouted, what I accused you of. It simply wasn't possible. How could you make a decision like that alone? Without my knowledge and against my will? Despite everything we'd talked about, everything we'd agreed? How could you lie to me like that?

"We can't have this child," I finally said, more softly, breathless after such a torrent of words. I tried to calm down. A doctor, I thought. We urgently needed a doctor.

"I'm going to call Rui," I said, and made to descend the staircase. But you ran a few steps down ahead of me and blocked my way, as if Rui was at the bottom of the stairs and everything would be decided the second I got there.

"I don't want you to," you shouted. You seemed changed, resolute. Ready to defy me, Rui Pais, and the rest of the world. "I don't want you to."

"What do you mean, you don't want me to?" I was furious. "You shouldn't have decided on something that doesn't only involve you. But if you get to decide things without me, I get to decide things without you."

Then I was watching you go tumbling down the stairs. I knew I'd shoved you just before you fell, I knew I'd held you against the handrail and shaken you by the shoulders, I knew you'd struggled and tried to break free, but I'd tightened my grip and pinned you to the handrail with firm fists, with my knees, I knew I'd struck out at you, at your belly, then pushed you down the stairs and you'd stumbled, when you reached the last step, and fallen to the floor, and stayed there on your knees with blood coming out from under you, staining your dress, as could be seen when you were stretchered into the ambulance, and I went in with you and sat beside you, the siren blaring, on the way to the hospital.

Your eyes were closed and you didn't say a word, as if you'd passed out. I cried silently, spoke silently, as if none of it was real, as if none of it was happening.

But it was real, it was happening, and that journey, with the heavy traffic and the chilling sound of the siren, felt like it would never end.

Things happened very quickly after that. They put you on a trolley straightaway and whisked you through the glass doors, and now they were asking me questions, making notes on a sheet of paper, and requesting your ID and other documents.

I sat in the waiting room or wandered the corridors. From time to time I went outside to smoke, then came back inside, sat back down, stood up again, not knowing what else I could do to cheat time. Eventually a doctor came to tell me that, if everything went according to plan, you'd be kept under observation for twenty-four hours and then released. And that we had, of course, lost the child.

He left and the first thing it occurred to me to do was sit back down and wait out those twenty-four hours right where I was. Then I realized that was absurd and went home. Or rather, I holed up at home, ashamed of myself, ashamed of having suddenly lost control, of having attacked you and then coldly carried on with the madness and the lies.

"She fell down the stairs," I told them at the hospital when they asked me what happened. "It was an accident. Yes, she was pregnant. Not long, about two months, we didn't know for sure. No, she was going to go to the clinic in the next few days, the appointment was made. When the accident happened."

And after lying with such conviction, there I was, on my own in the waiting room, alone with my thoughts and unable to lie any further. As if awaiting the verdict of some imaginary jury.

Or like an anxious father, nerves frazzled, awaiting news of his wife's health after she'd been rushed to the delivery room. A father? Had I been a father, even just briefly?

I went back to the hospital early the next morning, without changing my clothes, without having undressed even to sleep. I'd thrown myself onto the bed just as I was, at around two in the morning.

They let me see you. You were still asleep—they'd given you a sedative. I spent several hours at your side, watching you.

Eventually a nurse woke you up, gave you a warm cup of tea, and made you take some pills.

I took hold of your hand, but you didn't look at me. You didn't pull your hand away either, you just stayed perfectly still and stared straight ahead, as if you were dead.

The nurse sent me away while she administered some treatment and changed your clothes. When I came back you were laid out on your back again with your eyes closed, but I could tell from your breathing that you weren't asleep. That's how you were whenever I sat beside you, and I sat beside you almost the whole time you were in there. Sometimes you opened your eyes and stared at the wall in front of you.

You never said anything, never once spoke. But I hardly said anything either, because there was nothing to say. I wanted to spare you anything emotional or tiring.

I sat next to you, held your hand and pressed it to my lips, kissed you on the forehead or cheek, stroked your hair.

You never responded, but at least you knew I was there, that you could count on me, that I loved you more than anything in the world and that I'd never leave you, not under any circumstances. That's what my hands were saying as they stroked your hair and cheeks. They were also saying that we'd talk later, that I'd try to explain, that maybe you could forgive me. And that I'd never attack you again, no matter what. Never.

This dreamy, almost wordless atmosphere still held when I took you home some twenty-four hours later, put you to bed, brought you toast and a cup of milk as requested, and half-closed the shutters to dim the light as you shut your eyes, ready to doze off.

That was at five in the afternoon, and you didn't wake up until eleven at night, when you asked for another cup of milk. I told you what we had in the fridge, but you didn't want anything.

I'll go to the supermarket tomorrow morning, I said to myself, making a mental list of all your favorite things.

You were visibly pale and weak, but I'd look after you, I thought, tenderly arranging the bedcovers around your body. Just like you'd look after me, if it were me recovering instead of you.

So the next morning, I took you breakfast in bed and got ready to go out.

"I'm nipping to the supermarket," I told you eagerly, even joyfully. "What can I get you, besides the usual?"

"Nothing," you answered.

I kissed you on the forehead and said:

"I'll be right back."

As if I were talking to a child.

And I was quick. I whizzed round the aisles, scanning the shelves for things I thought you'd like. After all, I knew my way around the place—I used to do the shopping more often than you.

As I headed for the till, I noticed the florist and instinctively pushed my trolley over. Roses, I thought. A bunch of yellow roses.

"Twenty-three of these, please," I said to the florist, who thought I must have meant twenty-four and gave me an extra one. But I refused it and insisted:

"Twenty-three. One for each year."

And the florist smiled.

I entered the bedroom with the flowers in my hand. But you weren't there.

When I saw the unmade bed and your nightdress crumpled on top of the sheet, I took it as a good sign. You were feeling better, you'd got up and got dressed and were probably in the bathroom, or the living room, or kitchen.

But you weren't in the bathroom, living room, or kitchen. Or anywhere else in the apartment or studio. I called your name but there was no reply.

You must have gone to the bakery, the chemist, the fruit and veg shop, another nearby place. You'd be back soon.

I put the roses on the kitchen table and made myself a coffee while I waited.

But you didn't come back. As I drank the last drop, the sudden mad idea hit me that you might never come back.

I ran to the wardrobe. Your clothes were still there, hanging on their coat hangers, above the shelf for your shoes. I breathed a sigh of relief.

Leopoldo, I suddenly thought, and frantically began to search for him. Of course, you'd be with Leopoldo.

But the cat was nowhere to be seen either. He wasn't in the apartment or studio. And nor was the basket you used to carry him in.

Your notebooks, your drawings, your sketches, I thought in desperation. You'd have to come back for them. But your work shelves and drawers were empty.

That's when I knew you'd gone. You'd taken what was most important, Leopoldo, and your work and your notes. They were still part of your life.

You'd left everything else behind.

But I refused to believe my eyes. I argued against the evidence.

I could understand why you'd left me. There were valid reasons; you were extremely upset and angry. But surely it wasn't irrevocable. I loved you more than anything in the world, you knew that, and I knew how much you loved me.

We'd been happy together for four years, after all, which was more than enough time to test whether it worked. You shouldn't let happiness go once you've found it, because it isn't easy to find. You have to be lucky to find it even once. And I didn't want any other woman but you.

Your cousins' house in Estoril seemed like the obvious place for you to have gone. I must have phoned a thousand times, but they kept telling me you weren't there.

I spent days standing on the sidewalk outside that house, waiting for you to come out. But you probably saw me from the window and stayed inside.

I wrote you letters, which were never returned, but perhaps never read either. I phoned Maria Rosa, who seemed surprised. She didn't know where you were. If you contacted her she'd let me know, she promised.

Time went by without me noticing. I wanted to talk to you, even just once, to explain my side of the story. If you'd only hear me out, I was sure, you'd understand why I'd done what I'd done.

Finally, on my millionth call to your cousins' house, a woman's voice said impatiently:

"Accept it, she doesn't want to talk to you. Please stop calling."

She hung up, but I phoned right back.

"Please," I said.

But the voice cut me off.

"It's pointless, she's not here. She's not even in the country."

She hung up again, but I kept hold of the phone. I called a different number, asked about flights to London and booked myself onto the first one I could, the very same day. You must have been living back with your parents and studying at the Slade.

I phoned your parents' house as soon as I got to London, but to no avail. Another woman's voice, probably your mother's, gave me the same answer, day after day:

"She's not here."

I waited for you outside the Slade until one day I saw you—you were coming out, a file tucked under your arm. I rushed towards you, but when you saw me you turned away and vanished down a corridor. Frantically I opened door after door, but you weren't behind any of them.

For weeks on end I returned to the same spot, but I never saw you again. One day I thought I spotted you getting into a taxi in Sloane Square. I jumped into another cab and followed you through the streets, but always at a distance; we couldn't seem to get any closer, and then when we finally did catch up and I could see inside the window, I realized the woman wasn't you.

I started phoning again, several times a day, and eventually got a man's voice at the other end of the line.

"I'm Cecília's father," he said. And he arranged for us to meet in a pub at the end of the street.

I rushed straight over, jumping in the first taxi I found. Finally I'd have the chance to speak to you.

When I entered the pub I had the sensation that nothing around me was real. Nothing was real except my despair.

But I was ready to see you again. I'd have to weigh my words carefully, do whatever it took not to lose you. I'd give you time to think, I was prepared to wait as long as was necessary, until you'd finished your course at the Slade, anything. I'd do anything at all if it meant none of this was final.

I looked around the pub for you, but you weren't there. A man stood up and came over to greet me. Your father, who I knew only from photos.

It was a brief and civil encounter. We sat at a table where two glasses of whiskey were waiting, which we hardly touched.

"Cecília asked me to come and talk to you."

"Did she refuse to come herself?" I asked, already knowing the answer.

He nodded gently.

"I don't blame her. I deserve it."

Then there was a pause, a silence neither of us filled.

"But I also know she loves me," I said finally. "If she heard me explain things, she'd come back to me. That's why she refuses to meet."

"I don't think so," the man said coolly. "She's very resolute, she knows her own mind."

"But I love her more than anything in the world," I said, as if such a statement could overcome all obstacles.

"I've no doubt you're being sincere. But Cecília doesn't want to be with you. That's a fact and you're going to have to accept it."

I had my arguments ready, of course.

"The thing about what happened is—"

But he cut me off immediately.

"It doesn't matter now what happened, or who was to blame. It was a phase that's come to an end. Cecília has left you, and that's something you'll have to come to terms with."

He got to his feet not long after that, and I felt obliged to stand up too. Evidently, as far as he was concerned, the conversation was over.

But I couldn't admit defeat just yet. I wanted to say one final thing, but nothing came to mind.

Instead he spoke, calmly but firmly:

"She'll know how to get hold of you if she wants to. But I don't think that will happen. If I were you, I'd get on with my life."

It was raining outside. A typical London afternoon, a typical late afternoon in March, with a mist that took the edge off the street-lights and blurred the cars passing by. I thought about hailing a cab, but decided it would be difficult at that time of day in the rain. It made more sense to walk to the nearest tube station than wait on a corner under a dripping umbrella for a taxi that might never come. Besides, at that moment I felt like walking. When I reached the tube station at the end of the road, rather than going in I decided to carry on to the next one.

It occurred to me that I could continue walking, past one station, and another, and another, all the way back to my hotel. Not thinking about anything, not feeling anything, just listening to the rain fall on my umbrella.

I went back to Lisbon. The apartment was still full of you, and I half-expected you to walk through the door at any moment. After all, you still had a key. It seemed impossible that you'd have thrown it away; that you might, for example, have been walking across one of London's bridges and decided to toss it into the river. (It wasn't the Tagus you looked at anymore. It was a gloomier river, with darker waters, and banks so close together tourists would never mistake it for the sea.)

You still had a key. Maybe it was in your purse when you caught the tube, or in the handbag you placed beside you when you sat on a park bench. Because you'd sometimes sit down on benches in London parks, just as you used to here. It would no longer be in Graça or at the Senhora do Monte or Santa Luzia viewpoints, but in St. James' Park, for example, or Hyde Park, near the Serpentine.

Perhaps you'd pick up the bunch of keys and put your finger through the metal loop, wearing it like a ring. You'd hear the keys jangling against the metal without thinking of anything in particular, then you'd stand up and walk through the grass and fallen leaves. It was autumn.

And it was autumn in Lisbon too. Autumn linked us. Everything was the same yet also different: the weather, the city, the river, the sky, the light; all different.

Although the Greenwich meridian was only nine degrees and nine minutes away from Lisbon's. Or Lisbon was only nine degrees and nine minutes away from Greenwich's.

Meridians passed through places without anyone knowing. They could be used to measure longitude and calculate time. The time in London was the same as it was in Lisbon, and when you looked at the clock, you'd see the same time as I did. Midnight or midday in London was midnight or midday in Lisbon.

I acted crazy sometimes and went back to places I'd been with you, ate lunch in the same restaurants we used to eat in on Sundays. Trying to recover a time when you were there.

I went to that restaurant in Guincho, for example, where we'd sat at the table by the window looking out to sea.

When the waiter asked, "How many people?" I answered: "One."

But I looked at the seat opposite as if you might sit down in it at any moment. There'd been a minor delay of some sort, someone had phoned you with an urgent message just as you were leaving the house, you'd got held up in traffic, you'd gone to put petrol in Rui's car and there'd been a huge queue.

If you didn't show up it would be for some banal, comprehensible reason like that. Or for an incomprehensible but equally banal reason: because the flowers in the vase on the table were blue this time instead of red; because the napkin was folded the wrong way or had been placed upside down. Because there was different music playing. Because the wind had picked up and was blowing sand against the window. Because I'd had to sit at a different table and couldn't see the sea.

It wasn't fair to refuse to talk to me, Cecília. For your father to come and meet me instead, as if you weren't a responsible adult, as if you needed a representative, when really the opposite was true.

Were you afraid to see me? If you'd looked me in the eye would you have ended up coming back to me? Can a moment of madness not be forgiven when weighed against four happy years?

If you'd let me talk to you, you'd have reconsidered. You knew this and that's why you ran away, wasn't that right? Maybe with time you'd come to see things differently. Maybe you hadn't left me for good.

I waited for months for you, doing what I could to fill the time.

I found myself drifting around shopping centers, sneaking into cinemas. I'd walk out in the middle of the film with no recollection of what I'd just seen, not wanting to know whether it was day or night, summer or winter, staring blankly into shop windows, which seemed to be somehow all the same in the artificial light of the fake streets, varnished tiles on the floor and signs with absurd names on the walls. I lost myself in the crowds going up and down the escalators, people who devoured hotdogs or stood in queues outside cinemas, scooping popcorn into their mouths from huge buckets, desperate to while away a Sunday afternoon, to swallow up the tedium somehow.

I often slept during the day and woke up in the middle of the night. I got to know the places in the city that stayed open all night, or almost all night. I'd wander between bars, leaving when one closed and going into another that closed a little later or stayed open until dawn. I passed youngsters, in pairs or in bigger, noisier groups, coming out of nightclubs and going to get hot chocolate at Ribeira Market as day was beginning to break. I bumped into drunks who passed bottles around, vomited in corners, and pissed against walls. I walked on as if I hadn't seen, past beggars asleep in shop entrances or under bridges, laid out on cardboard.

And throughout it all, I never stopped talking to you in my head:

Was it out of pride that you sent an emissary to see me while you disappeared behind the clouds? Did you want to make yourself invisible, as if you were God? You wouldn't deign to speak to me, I wasn't worthy of addressing you, or even looking upon you—was that it? Was your invisibility a way of humiliating me—me, the sinner, before you, the confessor?

You exaggerated everything, Cecília, because really you were as much of a sinner as I was. It's true that I attacked you and that was wrong, but it's also true that you told lies to me and tricked me.

You betrayed me. You made a decision that wasn't only yours to make.

As if having a child wasn't a choice for both of us, as if it wouldn't suddenly change everything. It wasn't an insignificant step you could take on your own.

And what was I, then? A toy for you to play with, an instrument of pleasure, a mere object? How could you not consult me? You made a decision about my body without me— did you think you owned me? Did you think you owned the world? What on earth was going through your mind?

Were you imagining you could mold me, my life, and the world to your will?

Leopoldo had come first, like a practice run. (Is it possible that everything, even back then, was part of a plan?)

I said he couldn't stay and made repeated attempts to get rid of him. However, eventually he turned out to be useful for my art. I accepted having him around and even came to feel that he and I had a great deal in common. He became part of the household, part of the family.

There he'd be, all curled up, asleep in the last rays of sunshine on the rug or in his basket, while you sat there knitting; the pair of you enveloped in silence, a suspended moment within real time.

And while you sat there knitting, the months would roll by, and before anyone knew it there'd be a cot beside you with a child inside. A child for whom the cat had been clearing a path, as he silently padded across the rug, snuggled up in his basket, and went to sleep.

Until it would only take the slightest movement to push the cat a little to one side and squeeze a child in next to it.

Or so you'd decided, in the smooth way you operated. In the hypocritical, duplicitous way you operated. Confronting me with done deals, which I then had to deal with—to agree to—afterwards.

Convinced that you knew best. That everything in the world would bend to your will.

I salute you for your ability to manipulate me. You'd have made an outstanding puppeteer.

You shouldn't have tricked me over the child, Cecília. You left home having betrayed me.

All castles have a traitor's gate, including Saint George's. That's the gate you left through.

One night I sat down and started writing, and I didn't stop until I'd used up several sheets of paper.

Letter to my father:

I always thought I'd write you a letter one day, and now the time has come. I know it's too late, but that doesn't matter: even if you were here to read this, you wouldn't be able to understand it.

For a long time I felt that you loved us, just in a way I didn't really understand. But now I see things differently.

You were a mean-spirited man, utterly ignorant of generosity and affection. You liked to humiliate people, to trample on the most vulnerable, because it made you feel strong. Even as a bully you were a coward.

If you'd picked on your equals or superiors you'd have risked being beaten, in a real or symbolic sense. So you kept quiet in front of them, and unleashed all your hatred and anger on the weak. It was a kind of displacement, for I think the real target of your loathing was yourself. I recall the terrible scenes, the hysterical shouting fits, the uncontrolled rages and vicious tirades you subjected us to, and all for no good reason. Just because you could, and we were there.

It was three against one—me, my mother, and Alberta versus you—but we could never win, neither together nor individually. You were always stronger than us and we had to keep quiet, even when you were wrong, and the truth is you were always wrong. Even when you verged on being right, you undermined yourself by being so hostile, so out of step with reality. We were all afraid of you, but none of us respected you. Not even I did, and I was so little. Not even the maid, who used to mutter things behind your back that you certainly wouldn't have liked to hear.

My mother almost never spoke. But she sometimes defended me against you, which only made matters worse. I stayed silent too, letting the words build up inside me, to be said to you later on.

Back then I swore there'd be more than words. That I'd stand up to you, raise a fist, be prepared to attack. I'd pull a gun on you. I fantasized about this a lot, which was ironic given all your vain attempts to foster a love of guns in me. Well, I ended up taking an interest in them after all. I resolved to learn how to handle them, and as soon as I had, I'd shoot you.

At other times the dream ran in black and white, projected endlessly against a wall, on a loop: the figure of a man lying in bed, a door opens and in walks another figure who starts raining punches down on the figure in the bed. I was the figure who came in throwing one punch after another, and another, and another. And so on until the end of time.

Yes, I'd get revenge on you one day.

For a long time I thought I might win your respect with material success, because money was the only thing you valued. But after a certain point I knew that would never happen: you'd look down on anything I did, because you'd already decided I was worthless. If my pictures had fetched a high price, all it would prove was that society had gone to pot and there was no justice in the world.

You suspected there was a degree of pleasure in the creative process, and this would always diminish and tarnish my work in your eyes. True merit lay with laborers and peasants, who worked with their hands, like me, but with graft and for the benefit of everyone, not just the few businessmen or bank managers who had one of my pictures in their dining room.

That's what you always said—sometimes in words, and sometimes simply through your mocking laughter or sarcastic grin, as cutting as a razor blade.

No, when it came to me not even money would count. It wasn't real money to you if I was the one who'd earned it.

There was no point competing with you. I could never win. You'd change the rules halfway through or stop playing before the end. So I started ignoring you, looking down on you, forgetting you existed. I went to Berlin, wrote letters to my mother, but never sent you news. I no longer had a father, and you no longer had a son. I'd never really had a father anyway, and I tried to forget all about you. After all, I was an adult and I could look after myself.

Naturally, when you came to see me with your tail between your legs in the summer of 1980, to tell me you were broke, I couldn't believe my ears. I never thought, could never have even imagined, that such a sordid situation would give me my moment of triumph. I couldn't accept such a hollow victory.

I was horrified and thought you'd gone mad.

"You crazy old fool," I yelled, shaking you by the shoulders and pinning you up against the wall. I looked deep into your eyes and saw only fear and suffering, before a shadow fell across your face like a veil.

Senile dementia? I asked myself, looking at your shaking hands and empty stare.

Then I eventually found you at the roulette table, staring intently ahead, your hands atremble. You didn't even recognize me when you finally looked up, though I'd been watching you for some time from the other side of the table.

That's when I saw you for what you really were: a tramp, a gambler, a lost cause, a doddering fool. A nobody. You had no name, no memories, no family ties. No wife, no children, no past. You were not my father.

And yet I went over to you and reached for your arm.

"Come on, Father," I said. "Follow me."

You looked at me without recognizing your own son. And that's when I took you by the arm and forgave you.

"It's nobody's fault," I said, although you didn't understand what I was saying.

You let yourself be driven home.

Trying to see things from your point of view for once, I know you thought we abandoned you first. You thought you were the innocent one, you liked to play the victim. I'm sure you repeated your version of the story to yourself time and again:

Mother kept me away from you because she wanted my love all to herself. She belittled you in front of me and encouraged me to be wary of you. Lying and scheming, she turned Alberta, me, and the world against you, and everything I did wrong was ultimately her fault.

She was overprotective and this made me lazy. I lived in a dream world; I'd never be able to stand on my own two feet and serve society like a man. Maybe I wasn't even up to being a real man and loving a woman.

She ruined me, thinking she was loving me. She devoured me; I was the center of her world and she passed her hysteria on to me, locking me away with her in the attic and cutting me off from the world. I became a man-child in love with a woman. My own mother. It was a dangerous game and one that excluded you, my father, source of all things healthy and true, shutting you out while we went mad in our incestuous, fantastical world.

Because beneath her angelical appearance she was false and perverse, and despite her docile veneer she was fully capable of stabbing you in the back. An unsatisfied and quite possibly unfaithful woman, always looking to betray you. We'd formed a cabal against you, or rather she'd formed a cabal and made Alberta and me join. Knowing no better, as the years went by I'd come to embrace, internalize and identify with her way of thinking. She'd caused the breakdown between us.

So there you were. The victim.

You'd plucked that woman from her stuffy office and her humble, monotonous future as a typist. You'd saved her from that narrow life of poverty, you'd given her everything, made an honest woman out of her, and in return she shunned you, hid away in the attic, and turned your son against you. Your own son: so longed for and anticipated, whom it had taken two marriages to get and who was supposed to complete your life and brighten your world.

You had that paranoid way of seeing reality back to front, of turning yourself into the victim when you were in fact the assailant.

But now, as I write to you tonight, here in this empty house, I forgive your attacks. I forgive you for attacking us our whole lives.

I too have attacked, and I was far more violent than you.

I attacked a child. I attacked the woman I loved.

And so we found ourselves reversing the roles, Cecília.

You set off and I was left waiting for you at home. I was Penelope, waiting against hope, against all common sense.

But unlike her, I stopped waiting. I realized you weren't coming back, because nobody does. It's impossible to return: no one can bathe in the same river twice.

I realized I was mad to keep being faithful to you in your absence. Life was passing me by. The universe was in motion and I began to move again too.

I gradually unfastened myself, let go of the walls, the apartment, the canvas I worked on seeking you. I set fire to the canvas, the image I'd been weaving of your face, night after night, day after day.

Afterwards, again unlike Penelope, I burned, at least in my imagination, the bed where we'd made love, Ulysses' bed, built from an olive tree trunk, the bed that no one else knew except us. I made a bonfire out of it, lit it with a torch and watched it vanish into the flames. It burned for a long time, days and nights, and I watched, hypnotized, until it was gone. Something had ceased to exist.

I realized that if you did come back I'd sit facing you in silence, unable to communicate: the barrier of time would've come down between us.

Because a person can't return to the conjugal bed, make love, and tell of all that happened in the intervening years, with a goddess prolonging the night and postponing the day to make time for it all to be recounted, and for everything to go back to the way it was before.

None of that was possible, except in some fantastical tale.

We had left one another's lives, and now we each had our own life to lead.

So I accepted you weren't coming back.

One day when I woke up I was certain: you were never coming back.

And Lisbon disappeared with you.

It was an early November morning, the sun was shining and the wind blew cold, though really it was more of a sea breeze than a wind, and the sea itself was calm and the waves gentle, lapping rather than crashing onto the beach. And at Terreiro do Paço the old ferries came and went as usual, from one riverbank to the other.

I was the only one who could see it, Cecília, but Lisbon was falling apart. If I were to tell anyone else they'd think me crazy, but I assure you: Lisbon vanished when you did.

The earth trembled beneath my feet, houses bobbed up and down, swayed from side to side, for minutes that felt like centuries. Then roofs began to cave in, walls collapsed and a cloud of dust blocked out the sun. The streets could no longer be seen, but there was shouting and screaming coming from beneath the debris; everywhere people and animals fled, or were crushed by endless falling houses, or ran naked, barefoot, in nightgowns, out into the streets and squares; fires broke out in different places at the same time, people were dying, suffocating, burning, firemen couldn't get down the narrow streets, Baixa disappeared in flames and Chiado wasn't far behind. Lampposts fell, trees toppled onto cars and crushed anyone inside, people rushed out of their crumbling homes into streets which then opened up and became craters. Even in Campo Grande and out by the airport, where there were fewer buildings and many people had sought shelter, the ground parted and swallowed up sidewalks, trees, people, buses. Then the river burst its banks and rose, with the sea right behind it, and a giant wave engulfed Terreiro do Paço, reached as far as Rotunda and took everything with it, ships, boats, moorings, walls, houses, churches, crowds of fleeing people—

Lisbon disappeared with you.

But the time came to rebuild and I—as if coming back from the dead—began to dust myself off.

Take care of the living, I decided. Which meant me.

I opened the wardrobes and threw out all your clothes, because you'd never use them again. Not even the shoes I'd seen walk around the apartment so often with your feet inside, and which you sometimes slipped off to kneel on the sofa.

Your perfumes would never be worn again. They were still there, though some of them had evaporated, leaving empty bottles that still retained their aroma, still evoked you. Like the story of the spirit imprisoned in a bottle who escaped when an unsuspecting person removed the cap.

I smashed all the bottles and let your spirit out. Setting you free from the apartment, and setting the apartment free from you.

I wiped away every trace of you, until there was nothing left.

The place was now empty of your presence, of your shadow. Mine and mine alone, once more.

It was time to get on with my life.

CHAPTER III

City of Ulysses

I WAS FREE to go back to Berlin, to pick up where I'd left off. And that's exactly what I did, in April 1989, meaning I was there when the wall came down in November that year. For the second time in my life I found myself in the midst of a jubilant crowd celebrating freedom and the end of dictatorship, though it had been a very different dictatorship to our own.

I spent four years in Berlin. Then I did something I'd always wanted to do and took up residence in New York. I lived there until 2000, and in Los Angeles until 2003. I travelled to Japan twice from the US and got a bit of a feel for the place, though I was never there for very long. After that I wanted to go back to Europe, but not to Portugal. I moved to Milan and there I remained until the summer of 2008.

So I got to see a fair amount of the world, and naturally had a range of experiences.

Living abroad isn't always easy and, as is only to be expected, I ran into problems from time to time. But I can't say I found it difficult, or at least not unduly difficult, being so far away from home. I thought about it a lot, but I felt like millions of other Portuguese people, emigrants like me. Portugal is a country of emigrants.

Everywhere I went I lived among artists, many of whom were foreign, and together we formed a sort of community. I made some good friends, a few of whom I've kept in touch with over the years, and as far as I was concerned, that was all the community I needed. Deep down, I've never had much of a sense of belonging. I'd find it impossible, for example, to be part of a church or a political party, though I cared about social issues and expected high ethical standards, first and foremost from myself. But even when I was in Portugal, I'd always allowed myself to keep a certain distance, the freedom not to belong.

Looking back, it was a stimulating and productive time and I have no complaints. The sense of otherness you get from living in different societies forced me to see myself and my country in new ways, and this in itself made it all worthwhile.

I was doing what I'd always wanted to do. I'd established myself as an artist and achieved everything I'd set out to achieve: solo exhibitions, selling work to collectors and museums, gradually making an international name for myself.

Did any of it matter? Yes, in that it was what I'd always dreamed of. You could even say it was what I'd been born to do. What's more, I'd never compromised. I'd kept my artistic credibility and freedom intact, even if it did sometimes cost me in terms of sales and financial pressures. But I only ever did what I wanted to do and what made sense to me, and managing that while making a living was reward enough.

I had the occasional exhibition in Lisbon and stayed in touch with the gallery that gave me my first break, the owner becoming a friend as much as anything else.

I kept the studio in Graça too, though I didn't set foot in it myself for several years. Before going to Berlin I rented it out to Júlio Rocha and Simão, who'd been on the lookout for a place to work. (The rent they paid me, especially early on, helped me get to the end of the month without too much trouble. Because the financial side of things is never easy, though I'd learnt that already by then.)

Then, after speaking to the landlord, I passed the lease of the apartment on to Rui Pais. My place became the place where Rui and Manuela would meet.

Rui's request took me completely by surprise: he came to see me in 1989, when I was packing my bags and getting ready to leave, and told me his marriage to Teresa was falling apart and he'd become involved with another woman. It wasn't just a rough patch with Teresa, it was what he called a spent marriage; not finished, or even finishable, probably, because neither of them wanted that. Instead, it had become a sort of space they inhabited, which despite everything remained relatively comfortable, but where they failed to connect even when, or especially when, they made love. Teresa seemed fine with that, but he had since met Manuela, who was likewise married and in a similar situation. They were looking for a discreet place to meet. My apartment, once vacated, would be perfect.

It was a bolt from the blue. Rui and Teresa—I never would've thought it.

But I'd always been understanding of love's misadventures, mine and other people's. Some things are beyond our control, and it's not worth trying to rationalize them. We do what we can, for better or for worse. There's no point judging people.

I said yes to Rui straightaway, and even insisted on covering a few months' rent to pay him back for putting me up all those years ago.

It turned out to be a very convenient arrangement, because it meant I had somewhere to stay on the rare occasions I passed through Lisbon.

For a long time I avoided any sort of emotional involvement with women. All I wanted was sex. I let myself be drawn into wild parties, nights of drunkenness and excess after which I'd wake up next to women I didn't even know. I'd slip away while they were sleeping, with no memory of what had happened.

From that I moved on to having casual encounters, but more consciously and deliberately than before. There even came a point when I thought I was addicted to sex, but I wasn't particularly worried about it. There were worse vices, I thought, and, for me at least, this one wasn't destructive. Despite all the sex, or maybe because of it, I never stopped working. Women could be immensely inspiring, simply by existing.

Then came a phase in which I brought things down a gear and became more selective. Women began to interest me as human beings again, as people just like me, only of a different gender. They too had backstories, lives, sorrows, traumas, virtues and defects. I met all manner of women and seemed to have a strange knack for understanding them. Or at least that was the impression I got. I saw them for what they were, fragile beings unsuited to society and the world around them, but fighting with everything they had to stand on their own two feet. They built façades based on beauty, success or perseverance, and sometimes amassed alarming quantities of wealth and power. But very few seemed happy in their own skin. The women I knew back then lived on a knife-edge, with solitude a constant threat. They hid behind dark glasses and make-up, tried to disappear inside minimal clothing and stumbled over in their three-inch stilettos.

Such women came to me hoping I'd help piece them back together. I saw the enormity of what they were attempting, of what they believed, rightly or wrongly, was demanded of them: to work like mad and fight tooth and nail to achieve riches and success (whatever they understood as success), spending far too much on their appearance and eating as if they lived in the third world.

And the return they got on all this in terms of happiness was practically zero. I offered these women a kind of relief, a resting place by the wayside. A shoulder to lay their heads on, a receptive and convenient body, a reminder that there were antidotes to the setbacks and disappointments of life.

But they didn't serve the same purpose for me. I had no desire to talk about myself or reveal what lay beneath my surface. My skin was as far as they could go. Everything under my skin was mine and no one else's. I was a lone wolf, seeking only as much company as I needed.

Other women came along after that who I became more deeply involved with. There was Alison; our relationship began in New York and ended in Los Angeles, where she moved with me. But most of all, there was Benedetta in Milan.

Alison fell in love with me and my work, she seemed to think living with an artist gave her a certain allure. Deep down it was this imaginary allure she fell in love with and wanted for herself, maybe because she'd given up on her own artistic career.

She began to lead her life in such a way that it revolved almost entirely around me, as if she existed only to offer me support. She was becoming a logistics genius and insisted on taking care of everything, from catering and admin to public relations. She was one step away from telling me what I should paint and where and when I should exhibit. I tried to make her see the error of her ways. That living so vicariously through me would only lead to frustration, for herself and others. I had no interest in most of the things she considered essential, was perfectly capable of looking after myself and wouldn't accept any interference in my work. But she proved deaf to all arguments. Her presence became suffocating and I decided to break things off, as gently as I could, before it all got out of hand. Nevertheless, it wasn't an easy breakup, because she had such an irrational way of seeing things.

Breaking up with Benedetta was painful too, though less complicated in the end. She was an extremely beautiful and very successful businesswoman, and, unlike other women I'd known before, she was extremely comfortable in her own skin. She was divorced, mistress of her own destiny, and for a time we thought our affair might turn into something real. The only problem was that she was part of Milan's great social scene, with its constant parties, dinners, invitations, events. She was very much a part of this world, having been born into it and been immersed in it her whole life, and it seemed obvious to her that I'd now join her in it. It could only be of benefit to me, she said, I'd meet everyone who was worth meeting in the city.

But the glittering, luxurious world of Milanese high society and finance didn't interest me in the slightest.

Unlike her, I found it impossible to divide myself between intense but rewarding work, romance and sex, and glamorous parties. We came together in the middle ground, romance and sex, but this space slowly diminished once I decided no longer to enter the party terrain. I knew it was a fundamental aspect of her life and that if I cut it off I'd end up losing her. We split up after two years together, sad but clear-headed enough to accept that we were each of us the way we were, and would never change.

After that, I went back to Lisbon for a while, arriving in the summer of 2008.

Many years had passed, but my friendships remained the same. Friendship had always been a particularly stable part of my life, one in which I was loyal and resistant to change: we choose our friends and they choose us, and as the years go by we simply get closer.

Rui, who I'd been in touch with the most, had got divorced from Teresa, who had herself remarried. He'd moved in with Manuela, who'd also got divorced, and they lived in an apartment in Parque das Nações with a marvellous view of the river.

I temporarily rented an apartment in Graça, to be close to my studio, which had been returned to me for the time being.

Lisbon felt sad to me. It seemed to have lost its character, with huge banal developments springing up everywhere you looked. The newest part of town wasn't even worth a quick visit. It looked like a badly planned provincial suburb, sprawling out around giant shopping centres.

Rubbish collection was a disaster, the drains needed cleaning and the sewage system was inadequate. The pavements were crumbling, the roads were full of potholes, the parks had all seen better days and the buildings were decaying. Our national heritage had fallen into total disrepair.

The city was in the grip of an almighty social and economic crisis, though the government denied it every single day.

But it was there, it was visible, and it wasn't merely a symptom of a European or global downturn. It was a consequence of our own incompetence, of corruption and bad government, a lack of political will to fix the structural deficiencies that repeatedly surfaced.

I was looking for the Lisbon of seagulls, clear skies and the river, but I found a city of soup kitchens, homeless people and the unemployed, drug addicts on the streets of Intendente, beggars at every corner, a bare-chested lad with his head bowed and a can in his hand, kneeling on the pavement as if waiting to be scourged, blind beggars going up and down the metro, one tapping a tin box with an uncontrolled, jittery hand, muttering his litany: I'll be eternally grateful to anyone who has the goodwill or wherewithal to help me, I'll be eternally grateful to anyone who has the goodwill or wherewithal to help me, I'll be eternally . . . (meanwhile moving on into the next carriage, his voice ever more distant, until finally he could no longer be heard).

The hopelessness and sadness in the faces of passers-by. This wasn't genetic or endemic, it came from the realisation that those in power had betrayed us, and as ever we'd have to foot the bill. Whenever the country seemed poised to take a step forward, it ended up going backwards instead.

I didn't think I'd be in Lisbon for long.

I met up with Maria Rosa, who was still with Samuel. She was the only member of the old group I still hadn't seen.

She was the one who told me about you, Cecília, without me asking. You weren't one for writing, she said. At the most you might send a few photos or the odd line of important news, weddings or births.

That's how I found out you'd got married, in 1992, and had two daughters.

You'd remained in London until 1996, according to Maria Rosa, and now lived in Sweden, where your husband had been transferred, within the same company he'd worked for in London.

But it all seemed incomprehensibly distant to me, in both time and space.

A few months later I met Sara, and my life changed unexpectedly.

In a sense, she was a lone wolf like me. She wasn't afraid of solitude; in fact she sought it out, or accepted it as inevitable.

She followed her own path and didn't seem to be looking for anyone. She was levelheaded, confident and, above all else, utterly independent. I think that's what first attracted me to her, even more than her beauty. A cat-woman, I thought.

I found out, slowly (because she didn't like talking about herself), that she was a judge, that she'd had to overcome a great deal to forge a successful career, because she wouldn't be pressured or influenced by outside interests, and there were plenty of those around. The Portuguese legal system was a swamp.

She'd got divorced four years ago. It was an ugly business, because her ex-husband, a renowned lawyer, had been determined to drag it out and take her for all she was worth. He'd used every trick in the book, stretching the law to the limit but never breaking it. Which was precisely the sort of behaviour that had caused her to change her mind about him in the first place.

During their marriage, she'd come to realize that he wasn't the attractive and brilliant man she'd fallen in love with. From beneath his affable air and serene way of dealing with life, a different personality emerged, as if he'd been hiding it inside himself all along. This other version of him didn't distinguish between just and unjust causes; the difference between right and wrong depended entirely on what was most financially rewarding. He won most of his cases. He was a skilful operator and always acted lawfully, or rather, followed the law to the letter whilst completely betraying its spirit. This was common practice, of course, but she never imagined it would be common for him.

Eventually there came a day when she looked at him and saw a stranger. He wasn't the man she thought he was. She'd made a mistake and it was important to correct it. They'd never understand each other, so she no longer wanted him in her life. But he didn't want to lose her, and so battle commenced: he used every legal means at his disposal, as if he could somehow use the law to get her back.

It took me a long time to find most of this out. Sara didn't like talking about herself and she wasn't much given to dwelling on the past.

I picked up some of the details from the odd word or comment here and there, and gradually pieced the puzzle together. I'd have liked to have known more, I was fascinated, but I didn't want to intrude.

When I asked her questions, always casually and as if by chance, she gave me brief, fragmentary answers. Still, slowly but surely I got to know her, and the more I learned the closer to her I felt.

When I looked at her sitting before me, I hoped she'd one day work up the courage to speak, for I sensed a great buildup of tension inside her. But she seemed not to want to share it, as if her troubles, and by extension she herself, weren't important enough to worry about.

She, on the other hand, knew almost everything about me: I showed her all the pictures in the studio, including my portraits of Cecília, and told her the essential details about our relationship.

The paintings represented a significant stage in my artistic development, I told her. That was why I'd never wanted to sell them. They could serve as reference points in a retrospective one day.

She didn't believe a word of it, although she nodded along.

I realized I'd started to read her thoughts, and smiled.

I knew then that I'd end up becoming deeply involved with her. She'd entered my life in a way I didn't fully understand, and I had let her in.

Within a few moments I'd make love to her. Her beautiful feline body, as smooth as a cat's soft fur.

Love with her was as I'd imagined: intense and complicit. I felt she'd chosen me, just as I'd chosen her. Life is full of surprises, I thought. Even for a cynical lone wolf like me.

I was in a deep, close relationship with a woman for the second time in my life. And for the second time in my life I realized I'd be staying in Lisbon for longer than planned because of a woman. My nomadic side, which I liked to think had to do with me being a citizen of the world (but which was perhaps just my feckless side), shrunk into the background, or lay dormant, to be exercized for brief periods only. Preferably with you, Sara. But if you didn't want to, or couldn't, come with me, we both knew my absence would be short-lived and we'd soon be together again.

Life was full of nice surprises, I thought once more.

It was also the second time in my life that I'd fallen in love with a woman in Lisbon at a time when the city was in turmoil.

Unemployment was growing at an alarming rate, external debt was becoming unsustainable, there was no transparency in the public finances, the Bank of Portugal and other institutions hadn't properly evaluated our financial stability, the economy was stagnating, there was a lack of competitivity (which ministers pronounced "competivity" when they spoke on TV), the government proposed unnecessary or ill-timed public projects that would only aggravate the external debt and raise interest rates for generations, economic power was linked to political power, public-private partnerships mushroomed and secured deals that were ruinous to the public purse, the state apparatus grew unstoppably, the very logic of the system was irrational and out of control and the only possible solution to every problem was to cut salaries and bleed taxpayers dry. The small fry taxpayers, that is, because the big fish always escaped the taxman's net. Every day more and more middle class people slipped closer to the breadline, or fell below it.

But unlike in the 1980s, when the recession came on the back of a revolution and its turbulent aftermath, there were no excuses or mitigating factors now. It was time to face the consequences of our actions rather than blaming everything on the global downturn.

I watched you when we talked, Sara. Your flexible hands; long fingers, no rings. Your dark eyes, which sometimes became gloomy from one moment to the next.

Your professional life was demanding, in that you had to make high-level decisions on your own. The solitude of delivering judgements; the responsibility it entailed. And the tremendous courage with which you faced everything.

We had the same view on the causes of the crisis the country was going through; a combination of internal errors and an external recession. Because the crisis had hit Europe and the rest of the world as well.

They were times of upheaval, in which the old worldview urgently needed to be rethought and replaced. America had been (how strange to use the past tense) the richest and most powerful country on earth, it had placed its own interests above everything else and defended them by any means necessary. And now Wall Street had imploded and threatened to drag the western world down with it. We'd awoken to a rampant capitalism with no rules or ethics, selling fictitious financial products to the world. A small few earned millions, paid for by billions of other people. They might as well have been flooding the market with forged notes. And this form of corruption, which had spread like a cancer, was apparently deemed legitimate. The world was in a state of shock and would never be the same again. Was the unthinkable happening?

I admired your beauty, your principles, your character. And your sensitive, feminine, and immensely human side. Your capacity for passion and compassion.

Because I loved you I stayed in Lisbon, when anyone who could was emigrating.

But you refused either to emigrate or to conform. And I wanted to be with you and the many others who were working together in the hope that the country would wake up and change its ways. The way it saw itself and the rest of the world.

Three or four months later, Rui let slip, mid-conversation, that you were living in Lisbon again, Cecília. That your husband worked for a Swedish company and had been transferred here a few months ago.

I was surprised, but the news didn't strike me as especially relevant. I had no desire to see you. In fact I'd have preferred it if we never met again.

But we did meet, unexpectedly, at Miguel Luz's exhibition opening in May. I hurried around greeting people, planning to give Miguel a quick hug and then disappear because I'd never been interested in such events. Then suddenly a woman broke away from her group. Hello, she said, and I turned towards her.

Hello, I replied, and only then did I realise it was you. You were wearing a close-fitting black dress and a pearl necklace.

You smiled and said again:

Hello. As if there were no other words, or because no other words had occurred to you in those two seconds of silence.

But the next moment you were back in your group and introducing me to people, starting with your husband.

"Gonçalo Marques," you said. And then, turning to me:

"Paulo Vaz, whom I'm sure you all know." (Whom I'm pretty sure none of them knew. But I had no interest in getting to know them either.)

I gave them three or four lines of conversation and made my excuses. Miguel waved to me from the other side of the room, clearly pleased to see me, and after giving him the requisite hug, I was on my way.

It was a pleasant afternoon, the first signs of summer in the air.

Yes, summer was on its way and it was a lovely Lisbon afternoon.

I walked for a few minutes before reaching my car.

I hadn't recognized your voice when you first spoke. In truth, I wasn't paying much attention, and it was very noisy in the room. I only realized it was you when you turned around.

But I was totally indifferent to whether you were in Lisbon or not.

I had an exhibition in New York not long after that, then another in Tokyo. Sara went with me and both times we made the most of the opportunity to stay on for a few extra days. We came back from Tokyo towards the end of September.

And not once did I think of you during all that time.

Then in October I ran into you again, in IKEA. In the most improbable of places, in other words. In the most inappropriate of places. I must have said as much, for we both smiled.

The whole thing seemed absurd to me, beginning with our unnecessary attempts to justify our being there, me clutching a bag of light bulbs, you carrying duvet covers for your daughters, who were standing in a queue elsewhere in the shop.

The IKEA cafeteria was likewise the most improbable place for us to finally sit down together. But that's what happened. A few minutes after bumping into one another we were sitting at a table with cups of coffee before us.

"I've been following your progress, I always get the catalogues for your exhibitions," you said, and on seeing the look of surprise on my face, added: "It's easy enough to find them online, though sometimes I've ordered them direct from the galleries."

"And what about you?" I asked.

"I'll tell you some other time. In fact, I'd like to talk to you about it, if you get a moment."

Your mobile went off, a female voice, some friend you'd arranged to meet.

"I'm in the cafeteria," you said. "Come and find me here."

"Let's have a coffee in a proper place sometime and you can tell me what you've been up to," I said.

You passed me your phone and I copied your number into mine.

"Sounds good," you said. "You can't discuss fine art in IKEA."

And then you smiled again.

Your daughters suddenly appeared. The youngest must have been about ten, the other a little older. They were tall and very pretty, and I must have said something to that effect. They smiled, politely said something by way of reply, then went to buy drinks at the counter.

When they'd gone you said:

"I'm happy with my life and wouldn't change it in the slightest."

And a second later you added:

"But meeting you was the most important thing that ever happened to me."

When Leonor and Inês came back, each carrying a glass of juice and a Swedish cake on a tray, I said my farewells.

That unlikely meeting in IKEA, some time in mid-October, was the last time I saw you.

I spent the next two months struggling to deal with reality, not knowing quite when it had stopped being real. Part of me remained lucid and distant. Another part gave in to the irrational impulse to go back.

It mattered little to me that you now had another house, another man, who loved you and who you clearly loved back, two daughters who filled up your life and whom you loved so much you'd sacrificed your talent and let a part of yourself die.

You belonged to that house, to those three people, to the life you all shared. But another part of you lay in the shadows. You had repressed it, cut it off like an amputation.

And yet it might just have survived all those years of neglect. I could perhaps find that part of you once more, simply by dialling a phone number. Whether I saw you or not was no longer out of my hands.

I thought about calling you but kept putting it off, savouring the anticipation:

We'd meet in the bar of some classy hotel and tell one another what we'd been up to over the years. What we'd done, achieved, lost, dreamed; when it had been plain sailing and when we'd run aground; our triumphs and disasters.

And while we talked the daylight would hold and night would only fall when we'd told of all that had happened in the intervening years.

And afterwards, by some improbable miracle, the power of our words would have fused the past with the present and we'd exist together again, in the same city where we'd once been lovers.

We'd be able to travel back and revisit ourselves, if only for a moment. We'd have to deactivate our rational sides, disregard social conventions, commonplaces, and our overdeveloped sense of reality, and give ourselves over to the wondrous laws of instinct: our bodies would steer us past the humdrum obstacles of daily life.

You had another life now, but that was irrelevant as far as I was concerned. A part of you was coming back too, a part that had been lost up until now and only I could awaken. You'd slept for a hundred years, but there was still time to produce the works of art you carried inside you. Maybe you could even reconcile it all. Maybe at last, extraordinarily, implausibly, you'd manage to reconcile it all.

On the 20th of December I saw the story in a newspaper:

There had been an accident, probably caused by ice on the motorway. The car had come off the road and crashed into a tree. The driver had been injured, though not seriously, and the two girls in the back had emerged from the wreckage unharmed, but the woman in the passenger seat had been killed instantly.

The names, which I spelled out and pronounced repeatedly, unable to believe what I was reading, were the names of your family. The dead woman was you.

Reality had reached me by means of a newspaper. A reality I didn't know what to do with.

I read on and learned that the body was to lie in state in Santa Isabel church and then be cremated, on the morning of the 22nd, at Olivais cemetery. The ashes would then be scattered in the cemetery garden.

I didn't take part in any of that, of course. I had no right, your life and what happened to you was no business of mine.

It was also an easy way for me to pretend it wasn't happening.

I likewise refused to take part in any of the Christmas rituals of the next few days. I'd always hated Christmas, but that one was particularly awful.

Sara was planning to spend Christmas with her mother's side of the family, and I phoned to say I wouldn't be going with her. I'd explain later, I said, but I was boycotting Christmas this year.

I don't know if she understood.

I thought of taking myself off to a faraway country that didn't celebrate Christmas, somewhere Muslim or Buddhist, or any other religion, as long as I didn't know anyone. But picking a place and getting on a plane seemed like too much effort. I didn't have the energy for it, but I was also determined to avoid all company, no matter whose it was.

Sara called me on the 24th and 25th but I didn't pick up. Instead, I recorded a message on my answering machine and an out-of-office on my email saying I was away travelling, then secretly stayed exactly where I was.

I couldn't accept losing you when I'd been so close to seeing you again; when you'd been just one phone call away.

Now the moment had passed forever. And because it had

never happened, I tried to imagine it. I wondered what you'd have told me, how you'd been for all those years, what the views had been like from your house, from your various houses, in London, Sweden, Lisbon.

(Guided Tour of Your House.)

I thought of asking Maria Rosa for photos of you, but I dismissed the idea. She'd have thought I was mad.

I found myself wanting to gather all the traces of you I could find, whatever form they took: stories, testimonies, photos. And whatever I couldn't find, I'd have to invent. I wanted to know what your house was like in Lapa, to go up in the lift, push open the door and step inside, leaf through family albums, see you in photos with your kids, piece together your life on the outskirts of Stockholm, imagine what you'd done, how you'd spent your time, what books you'd read, what music you'd listened to. A wife and mother busy with domestic duties, going to Swedish classes, as was more or less compulsory for foreign residents, taking her daughters to school and picking them up—daughters who spoke Swedish better than she did, who spoke Swedish as a third language, their second being English, for they'd been born in England and only spoke Portuguese at home, and who now, living in Lisbon, went to St. Julian's, because it was important to keep up another language, since after all they might end up living anywhere.

I wanted to recover an instant with you, as if in doing so I'd somehow recover a part of myself. I couldn't accept that things would be left the way they were at that moment: as an unfinished conversation.

It was around then that I received the invitation from the director of CAM and, after a fair bit of hesitation, decided to put on the exhibition I'd thought up with you. I've been working on it for several months.

Now you'd leave your house in Lapa and sit in the studio while I worked, just as you used to.

It was easy for me to bypass reality, to ignore it and subvert it. To love a person is to speak to them even when they're not there, someone once said.

Because we carry that person within us. They become a part of us, something vital only we're aware of.

Years ago, I would often imagine going to get you, going up the stairs or taking the lift, breaking down the door to your apartment and dragging you out by force, carrying you away with me even if you didn't want to come.

But now you came of your own free will and sat down in your usual place.

And now, just as I had done years ago, I stared at your empty chair in the studio.

I asked myself what it would've been like to have spent my whole life with you. If it was your absence that made you so unique, because my imagination made you larger than life.

I knew what you would've said:

"It's easy to be the greatest of lovers if you're separated by sea or death."

Ulysses loved Penelope more than anything in the world, so long as there was an ocean between them and he could have all the women he wanted, you'd say. Seeing things as clearly as ever.

Would I have been unfaithful to you if we'd stayed together? I may have been, but I'd have covered my tracks so you never knew. You would never have bought the idea that infidelity didn't matter. Nobody really believes that.

If I'd been unfaithful to you, it would've been to prove to myself that I wasn't reliant on you (when the truth is I was emotionally reliant on you, though I don't think you ever knew that).

But maybe I wouldn't have been unfaithful. I was happy with you. You didn't suffocate me; you occupied your own space and never deliberately occupied mine. You gave me freedom, you weren't jealous or possessive or nosey, you didn't ask questions, you weren't anxious or insecure. You were simply there, serenely occupying your space. As you saw it, love was perfectly simple, unchanging, resistant to day-to-day life. You weren't afraid of wear and tear or getting old. As the years passed, you'd continue to focus on us and your work. Nothing essential would change.

It's true that, to a large degree, my relationship with Sara is like that as well. Or at least it was, until you showed up and drove a wedge between us, then disappeared again and left me reaching for you in the dark. This is the second time in my life that you've suddenly disappeared—you have an unbearable habit of disappearing, and it's something I'll never be able to accept. I'm still in mourning for you. And Sara, who I've talked to about it, knows exactly what I'm going through.

If we'd stayed together, would you have been unfaithful to me? I'd always thought not; you were happy and had nothing to prove to yourself. If you'd been unfaithful to me, would my world have collapsed? I think I could probably put up with the odd infidelity, provided they never lasted. No, I wouldn't have said anything. I'd have tried to ignore it, waited to see what you decided to do. But I never thought there was any danger of this; I was sure of your love for me.

Especially because I gave you what you most wanted: the chance to be yourself. I was the exception. According to Benedetta, men can forgive women anything, even an affair, absolutely anything at all, except talent.

But I admired and loved your talent, Cecília. And I didn't compete with you, because I was also so sure of my own. We could be free and walk together side by side. The same and different. The perfect pair, Le Couple.

It's not true that I still love you only because I've lost you. I also loved you deeply when I had you. My love for you was never Pedro's love for Inês. My Eros has never been the doleful sort, as he often is in this country of melancholics. Ours wasn't a typically Portuguese form of love.

I realized (it was Alison who taught me) that men are easily loved for their work, talent, reputation, and career. But it's very rare for a man to fall in love with a woman because he admires her, because of her talent, because of the work she creates. Maybe I was an exception to this.

But having begun this game of going back and looking at Lisbon with you again, Cecília, I've come to the conclusion that I don't want to, or cannot, recover our project after all. I'd rather not touch it, I'd rather let it remain what it always was: disconnected ideas tossed into the air, to the mercy of fate and the wind.

So I decided to do something else, something different: blurred images of Lisbon, in which the city could be guessed at more than it could be seen. Because Lisbon wasn't put under the spotlight or paid any attention by the rest of the world, people's image of the place was slightly out of focus. I'd therefore offer an oblique vision, somewhat squinted, and false, forcing viewers to look again, a second and a third time. Pictures that challenged viewers to inspect them more closely, that promised to disclose more than first met the eye, and made people want to see more. Lisbon emerged as a desirable city, a city you had to find for yourself.

A few weeks or months later, while we were cooking dinner at my place, Sara suddenly stopped mid-sentence and, after making a failed attempt to contain herself and finish what she was saying, turned away from me and burst out crying. She shed rivers of pent-up tears, although she tried to hold them back when I hugged her, burying her face in my shoulder.

I let her cry, not saying anything, just hugging her.

Then all at once she looked up and said: something's on fire. There was smoke everywhere, obviously coming from the burnt food.

"Never mind," I said, quickly switching the flame off and plunging the frying pan under cold water, which made even more smoke, enveloping us in a thick fog.

I opened the window and sat you down at the table.

"I'll make an asparagus omelette instead," I said, as cheerily as I could. "My speciality."

She smiled and then said:

"It's all the stress. Sometimes it gets the better of me."

And she talked of pressures at work, the threatening messages people sent her in the post or via text. But I knew that wasn't it, though it was more than enough for anyone to cope with. What was upsetting her was our relationship. Her defences were down and she'd realized she was vulnerable and alone; she'd suddenly found a man who loved her, but he was suffering because he'd lost another woman. And he was a lone wolf. He put his work before everything else and loving him would probably never amount to more than this. Which at that precise moment felt like next to nothing.

That's what I heard, inside me, while she spoke of other things.

A strong woman, but fragile too, even helpless.

A woman who was different from other women, unique. I hugged her again. I'd stay with her, by her side, defending her against all the threats and blackmail in the world. I wanted to carry on and tell her I loved her, admired her, had chosen her, wanted to be with her. But I was afraid of myself, afraid of saying too much. I didn't want to make things worse by not living up to my words.

I felt vaguely as if I were sleepwalking, removed from time, in a kind of interval in my life.

We talked the next morning. I needed space to think and re-connect with myself, I told her. This was a dark time, a period of mourning I had to get through and deal with.

I know, she said. You need to be alone right now.

She proposed that we not see each other again until after the exhibition, and I agreed.

I went for a walk down by the riverside, watched a bicycle slowly pass over a poem written in white on the tarmac: *The Tagus is more beautiful than the river that flows through my village.* The wheels rolled along the tarmac, eating up one word after another, beginning slowly and then gathering speed, and I listened to the sound of the wheels turning over the words, still legible at first but then sliding into one another, becoming confused, until eventually they were nothing but a blur.

Writing as an image, the legible and the illegible as the front and back of a mirror, words reflected or projected onto the water,

the tarmac of the dock turning into water, the words turning into the river, the words *From the Tagus to the world* bobbing along in the river and then seamlessly entering the sea, where the water rises and falls, burrowing into itself, becoming a deep blue, while the white letters darken into black, and begin to come apart in the water until they can no longer be read.

I had various paintings ready and was working on the last two.

Only the odd trace remained from our original project, such as the name of the exhibition (*"City of Ulysses*, an exhibition by Paulo Vaz, based on a project by Cecília Branco") and the tagline we'd thought up years ago:

"Tourists go away to escape from themselves and only care about real cities. But travellers go in search of themselves and prefer imaginary cities. With a bit of luck, they find them. At least once in their lives."

The exhibition had already been advertised in the papers, and the opening would be in two months' time.

It occurred to me (why hadn't I thought of it before?) that the notebooks you drew and wrote in had perhaps survived your various moves, from country to country, house to house. Perhaps there would be something in one of them connected to the theme, which I could use or at least reference in the catalogue.

I ought to call your husband, arrange to meet him and talk about it.

But it was two o'clock in the morning. I decided to wait until the next day.

Remarkably, it was Gonçalo Marques who phoned me the next morning. He'd seen the advert in the paper and wanted to ask me about it. He could come by my studio whenever was convenient.

"I wanted to ask you something too," I said. "In fact, I was just about to call you."

We arranged to meet the following day, at his office, which was relatively close by.

His office was comfortable, if impersonal, and situated on the top floor of a high-rise block. A large window provided a broad panoramic view of Lisbon.

He got straight to the point:

"I read in the paper that your exhibition is based on a project by Cecília Branco."

"That's right," I said. "Years ago now, we came up with the idea of an exhibition about Lisbon. I've ended up doing something different, but I kept the title and tagline."

"Then it's your exhibition. Cecília's name is merely mentioned."

"That's what I wanted to talk to you about," I said. "I wanted to ask whether, by any chance, she left anything—pictures, papers, notebooks or whatever—that might be relevant. If she did, I'd like to try and include them, or at least reference them in the catalogue."

He was silent for a moment.

"There's a lot more than that," he said eventually. "That's why I phoned. Cecília left loads of pictures, prints, drawings and sketches, and hundreds of notebooks. There are also videos, film reels and thousands of photos."

I looked out at the city sprawling towards the horizon and ignored Gonçalo's presence for a moment. I wanted to be alone with what he'd just told me.

Then I turned to him:

"That's the best news I've had in years."

I looked at the outline of the city again, beyond the glass, and switched off. I suddenly realized he'd started talking again:

"As for the advert in the paper, I wanted to tell you that an exhibition of the same name, *City of Ulysses*, is described and mapped out in Cecília's notebooks. There were even several paintings done for it. She'd been meaning to tell you, seeing as the project was originally also yours."

He took another pause. I didn't fill it, so we were both silent for a while.

(*"City of Ulysses*, an exhibition by Cecília Branco." The phrase appeared in my mind as if I'd seen it somewhere before, perhaps on a poster. I could see it, picture it.)

"If Cecília planned it, the exhibition should be hers. I'll give the space over to her and remove my name."

He repeated my words, as if not believing them:

"Remove your name?"

"Perhaps I'll add it again later. I don't know, it doesn't matter. I'll remove it for now."

Then I added that if he agreed, I could arrange the hanging of Cecília's exhibition. After all, I had plenty of experience.

Again, he looked at me surprised.

"In fact, that's exactly what I was planning to propose: that you drop your exhibition for now and do Cecília's instead," he said, and I noticed his voice soften, as if in relief, as if he'd been expecting me to put up a fight.

"When can I see Cecília's work?"

That was all I needed to know, then I could leave. The meeting was over as far as I was concerned, and I made to stand up.

But Gonçalo seemed to have all the time in the world. He gestured for me to remain seated.

"Her notes and instructions are often quite fragmentary," he said. "The exhibition isn't planned in such a way that it could be put together by technicians alone. It will take more skill than that, the input of someone with experience in gathering disparate pieces and making a unified whole. So I'm grateful for your offer to help set it up."

He paused briefly before continuing:

"Cecília trusted you. She put it down in writing, years ago, that if anything were ever to happen to her, all her unfinished work was to be handed over to you. You'd know what to do with it."

Her entire artistic output had been photographed and scanned. He'd been planning to phone me about it soon, but then he'd seen the advert in the newspaper and realized there was no time to lose.

I could go and see her work whenever I liked, he said, and then we could discuss things in more detail.

We agreed I'd go to his house the following evening, and that was the end of the conversation.

And then I was going up in the lift and entering your home, Cecília, and I found you everywhere, in the photos on the wall, in picture frames on side tables, in certain paintings, which even from a distance I could tell were yours, and to which my eye periodically returned. You were there, in the cheerful, welcoming atmosphere, the way everything fitted together, the arrangement of the furniture, the choice of ornaments, the soft folds in the curtains.

(Guided Tour of Your House.)

But it was a part of your life that had nothing to do with me, where you were simply "Mum," or the wife of that affable man who pointed me to a sofa and offered me a glass of port.

"Cecília was planning to put on an exhibition in Lisbon soon," he said, leaning over to pour from a cut-glass jug. "In all the years I knew her she'd never wanted to exhibit her work, apart from in the odd collective exhibition in London. She didn't have much time, of course, when the children were little. But whatever else was going on, she never stopped painting."

I stared at the nearest photos, arranged on the side table beside me: you with a child in your lap, you holding two children by the hand, one on either side, dressed in matching berets and kilts, somewhere in the English countryside; you on a London street; you sitting on a garden chair outside a wooden house surrounded by tall trees, almost certainly in Sweden.

On the opposite wall, above the sofa, were paintings of yours, which your husband then showed me: *Girls and Cats; Self-portrait with Umbrella; Portrait of Gonçalo; Seated Woman.*

As I looked at them more closely, I smiled. I knew you wouldn't disappoint me, Cecília. If I'd ever had my doubts— and I never had—here was the proof.

I looked at the signature in the bottom right corner and could almost see your hand writing it. Underlining it, as always, with a little dash.

You'd studied engraving for two years at the Slade with Bartolomeu, Gonçalo said. He admired your work a lot. Not just him, everyone. But in London you'd only ever been part of group exhibitions, you'd wanted to have more work finished before thinking about a solo show. Then came Sweden and the children, and it was only recently that you'd started planning your exhibition.

He showed me prints hanging on the wall in the study, and oils and acrylics in the dining room.

Then we went into a studio that had a huge window with views of the river. Night had fallen and the bridge was lit up, with more lights beneath it, boats perhaps, and more on the other side of the river. This was where you'd worked: your easel was still there, and the wicker chair you sat in, with a high back where you could rest your head. There was a dark sofa pushed up against the wall, piled with colourful cushions, and a hand-woven rug on the floor.

I saw the paintings of the saints in the June street parties, based on the sketches you'd shown me all those years ago. And photos of the children, photos of you and your husband in Sydney, New York, Singapore, Athens.

Gonçalo opened a folder full of drawings; he showed me a series of canvases stored inside a cupboard; he opened drawers containing hundreds of notebooks. Then finally we came to the folder of unfinished work you'd asked to be delivered to me.

It must have been one o'clock in the morning by the time I'd finished looking at it all.

"I think there ought to be two exhibitions at the Gulbenkian at the same time," I said to Gonçalo, who'd been watching me and trying to gauge my reaction. "*City of Ulysses*, and then another with the rest of the work. To show Cecília in two different lights."

(From one day to the next. Cecília Branco.)

And naturally there was enough material to do a great deal more as well.

"I know," Gonçalo said. "Books, for example. A book of her work. A photo biography. Publishing her notebooks. Further exhibitions, thematic or chronological."

"There's enough to keep a lot of people busy for a long time," I added. "People are going to want to study Cecília's work. The Gulbenkian exhibitions will just be the start. I'll talk to the director of CAM about the idea of doing two exhibitions. He'll want to see the work and speak to you, of course. If you don't mind, I'll give him your contact details."

Gonçalo agreed, then gave me the folder intended for me, and various CDs and DVDs.

"All her work is here, scanned, including the notebooks and her plans for the exhibition, plus some films and videos. I think it's enough to be getting on with. But call me if you need anything."

I told him I'd start by looking at everything relevant to *City of Ulysses*, then said goodbye and promised to be in touch soon.

In the lift, as soon as it began to descend, I felt strangely dizzy and realized I was exhausted. When I reached my car and opened the door, the only thing I could think of was that somewhere in that apartment where you no longer lived, in a room I obviously hadn't entered, two children were asleep.

I spent the rest of that night, and the days and nights that followed, going through the CDs and DVDs and the unfinished work. I drank coffee whenever tiredness threatened to get the better of me, but I didn't lie down or sleep.

I wanted to follow you on your journey, Cecília. And above anything else, it was you I was looking for in the work, the footage, the photos. In a life I never knew.

In a London park, in the Swedish countryside, among trees in autumn colours or fields full of snow, landscapes you'd later worked on in paintings. Your house in the Stockholm suburbs. Your children growing up, like in the pages of a family album. A dog on the lawn. Dusk and the white light of winter.

Now you were talking to the video camera, and I recognized your voice.

But I lost track of what you were saying—it must have been four or five in the morning by then before picking up the thread again a few phrases later.

(Guided Tour of Your Paintings.)

All I had to do was follow you, follow your voice. You talked about what inspired you, and how some of the pieces had come about.

But that wasn't the most important part. I'd follow you, wherever you went, down paths into your tiny world, which would grow into a larger world of other people, the violent, chaotic, and incomprehensible world we all inhabit. I'd follow you as you attempted to make sense of the absurd, to organize the chaos, to find harmony where none existed.

I'd look for you as if piecing together a jigsaw, wading through a variety of different materials, forever tempted to submerge myself and abandon my bearings.

But I mustn't lose my bearings. I wanted to learn everything I could about your journey and your context, but I didn't have much time to organize the exhibition and I wanted to present you to the world in the best way possible; to help you, help your name, become known throughout the world. Cecília Branco.

Only on the third night did I lie down and sleep.

I woke early and phoned Sara, whom I'd kept informed of the developments, and then rang the director of CAM: I urgently needed to speak to him, there'd been a change of plan.

He told me to come straight over. In his office he listened carefully to what I said, surprised at first, then delighted when I described the extent of the work and outlined Cecília's exhibition in greater detail.

"Does it overlap at all with what you'd planned to exhibit?"

"No, I ended up preparing something else, a different project entirely."

They'd place a new advert in the papers to say that *City of Ulysses* would now be an exhibition by Cecília Branco alone, he said. But I'd have to explain all this to the press, and soon, before the new advert came out. Such a radical departure from the original plan couldn't come out of nowhere.

And my exhibition would have to follow Cecília's, he said. It would mean changing the dates of all the other exhibitions that year, but he insisted.

"That's fine with me," I said. "My exhibition's all ready to go, after all. I'll just have to change the name."

I gave him Gonçalo Marques' phone number and he said he'd ring him right away. He admitted to being extremely curious to see the work.

Later the same day, I gave the Gulbenkian press officer an announcement to send out and thought that would be that.

Two days later, the director of CAM phoned: he loved Cecília's work and agreed to two simultaneous exhibitions. He'd take charge of the second one, contracting a curator and team to assemble everything in record time.

I was overjoyed at the news, and arranged to send him the unfinished work as well. It was fascinating in itself, I said, and fundamental to the context. Then I got back down to my own task.

I never anticipated the media storm that followed, involving several newspapers but led by countless mass-distribution magazines. I had to change my mobile number, disconnect everything else, use my phone only to speak to Sara and be otherwise uncontactable. But before that, I'd received a torrent of questions and urgent requests via text and email:

Who exactly was Cecília Branco? What role had she played in my life? What was my involvement with her? How and when did we meet? Did we ever work together? Were we lovers? What were our family backgrounds? How did the idea for *City of Ulysses* come about? Why that title? Why had I stopped collaborating with Cecília? What sort of life did I lead? And what sort of life did Cecília lead? How had she died? What did her death mean to me? How did I feel about her now? Why was her exhibition happening instead of mine, even though mine had been announced first? Was I trying to plagiarize her? Had I tried to steal her project and pass it off as my own, now that she was out of the way?

Or, alternatively, why on earth would I, an internationally renowned artist whose work was all ready to go, give up the inaugural spot in a major exhibition series to a total unknown? Was it all a game, a deliberate attempt to confuse people, a promotional gimmick?

Why was I interested in Lisbon? Why had Cecília been interested in it? Did I not think Lisbon was a dilapidated city, dirty and abandoned, the victim of a succession of council administrations that had failed it, betrayed it, destroyed it, and stripped it of its character? Did I not think the interests of private developers dominated everything and had led to some real atrocities being built in the city? Did I not think the modern neighbourhoods were eyesores and the suburbs were terrifying? Did I not agree that the Parque das Nações, though a good idea at first, had been overdeveloped? And was I aware that the council planned to alter town planning laws in order to build on public spaces, even in historic neighbourhoods?

These last questions I'd be happy to answer. But only after Cecília's exhibition.

I stopped reading emails. I'd go through them all later and answer any worth replying to.

The last message I read, which I obviously didn't respond to, despite the author chasing me, by various means and with incredible persistence, said the following:

"I'm a young trainee journalist looking for a story, and I've a feeling there's a good story behind this exhibition. That's why I'm writing to request an interview. And believe me, I'm prepared to do anything to get it, even if you refuse. Don't underestimate my powers of perseverance and persuasion. As you'll know, some journalists spend their entire lives following stories through to their conclusions. And that's what distinguishes a good story from an okay one: a journalist prepared to put her life on the line to get to the bottom of it."

I knew, from having spoken to him, that Gonçalo was as besieged as I was, and that he too had made himself uncontactable. The statements he issued via the Gulbenkian press officer gave as little away about his private life as my statements did about mine.

The truth is, the general public don't particularly care about art, books, and ideas. But any whiff of gossip or controversy in a person's private life is sure to spark curiosity and get pulses racing, leading to a swathe of television appearances and contradictory newspaper articles, and consequently overnight fame, box office success, and a rush on ticket sales. It was therefore common for some outrage or provocation to be contrived, with varying degrees of skill, to generate publicity. Any justification sufficed, or no justification whatsoever, so long as it was divisive or touched on a raw nerve.

But none of us would ever play this game or try to take advantage of it. Not even the director of CAM or the Gulbenkian, however much they wanted the exhibitions to be a success.

It gradually became clear to me how best to organize your show, Cecília, based on the plans and instructions you'd left. I was even going to include extracts from the Notebooks, to expand on certain ideas or enable them to be seen in a different light. The pages of the Notebooks would be turned virtually, by a movement of the visitor's hand.

I won't describe the exhibition to you in detail for you already know it from the inside, having imagined it over the years, at different points in time, in different places.

I'll merely tell you how I arranged anything that you'd left unresolved, and, just like we used to do with one another's work,

I'll pick out a few aspects that particularly interested me. For example, writing as seduction. We worked in the visual sphere, but writing had always seduced you and drawn you towards it like an abyss: words were there to be read, they established or animated worlds. (Which is why I included extracts from your notebooks.) I understood why you'd focused on engraving for a while: the desire to leave a trace, a sign of your passing, like a furrow through time.

You produced prints of an imaginary Lisbon and covered them in words, like a body you were making love to.

In several of these prints—a hill, the castle, the river, fields leading down to a beach—other people's words appeared, and by including them you made them yours:

"fertile soil,"

"trees and vines,"

"goods of all kinds, of the finest quality or for everyday use."

"The olive tree thrives."

"Many species of game."

"Hot baths."

"We have silver and gold."

"Lemons too."

"An abundance of figs."

"Grass grows even in the squares."

Twelfth-century Arabic Lisbon was a bountiful city too.

"At the time of our arrival, it was already the most opulent commercial centre in all of Africa and much of Europe."

The Tagus was "two thirds water, one third fish." "Gold [. . .] can be found in the Tagus," said Pliny, and according to Ovid: "The Tagus flows / With molten gold instead of water." (The gold in the Tagus lasted until the sixteenth century.)

And there was the series of paintings, almost all of them acrylics, that you called *Ulysses*, but which might equally have been stories from Portugal's past: *Woman at the Window, Woman*

Waiting at the Window, The Wait.

(In this last one, time stands still on the faded face of a clock; there are flowers in a vase on a table and a woman is sitting with her hands on her lap, an open book before her. Her gaze is fixed, staring into the void. The void, or death, is the subject. The painting is a still life.)

And others too that depicted solitude, abandonment, melancholy: a woman gazing out to sea from a deserted beach; a woman sitting in a vast empty field.

From the *Stockholm Notebooks*:

The silence of forests. Wide, unpopulated open spaces, a form of beauty that is in its way oppressive. Silence as a suspended moment, before a scream. I listen, waiting for the scream to come.

But nobody screams.

Heavy silence accumulates on the trees, fields and paths, in thick layers of overlying snow.

And there were the vastly enlarged photos of footprints on a beach, the bare feet of a man walking. (I remembered them. One morning in Tróia.) The mythical footprints of Ulysses.

From the *London Notebooks*:

Trip to Greece with Gonçalo. A real trip, documented and dated, but also symbolic, seeking roots. I kept the plane tickets, London-Athens-London, museum passes, restaurant and hotel bills, the tickets from the ferry that took us round various islands, from the boat we caught to Crete. I brought back drawings, sketches, notes, sometimes scribbled on loose scraps of paper; maps, old postcards, photos.

Some of these photos were entitled *Mediterranean* and across them, or in captions placed underneath them on the wall, you'd written the first verses of the *Odyssey: Tell me, oh muse, of that artful man who wandered far and wide after abandoning the sacred*

walls of Troy.
And a sculpture suggesting a woman lying down, onto whose body a map of the world was intermittently projected.

From the *Stockholm Notebooks*:
All men's travels ultimately pass over the body of a woman, or many women.

Ulysses encountered many women, including Circe and the Sirens, but he returned to the first, the one who stayed at home, weaving both of their stories.

In Ithaca, Penelope wove Ulysses' return.

A glass box, which you called *The Enigma* and which was shaped like a diamond, filled with water, sublimely blue; an amazing, blinding colour. It was less a drop of sea than an example of blue in its purest state, a dazzling blue that seemed to come from another dimension. Sparkling under a spotlight, it became a boundless object. Or maybe even desire itself, with no object; the seduction of the unknown, that makes us leave our lives behind and set off in search of adventure.

(A specific amount of aniline had to be inserted into the box every day to keep the blue constant, I informed the technical team.)

From the *London Notebooks*:
In Greece I was seeking the Mediterranean spirit; affinities with another country on the edge of Europe, southern and backward, with striking contrasts between light and shadow and a vertiginous past containing ancient civilisations.

I found the same vegetation and the same Mediterranean climate as we have south of the Tagus: rugged landscapes, dusty paths, arid white earth, heaths of rock-rose and heather, mules, steep inclines, ruined windmills, herds of goats, green-grey olive trees, poppies. And extensive vines, for we, like Greece, have been a country of wine and olive oil for thousands of years. And we, like Greece, have always looked out to sea.

Lisbon is an Atlantic city, but with a Mediterranean configuration: a bay that provides a natural shelter beneath the hills, like the Acropolis in Athens.

Lisbon followed me, as Cavafy wrote of Alexandria.

I sought deepest Greece, I took photos and made rough sketches: cottages, limestone plateaus, the exaggerated blue of the sea and sky, the exaggerated white of the houses, fishermen, an old lady sitting on the doorstep sewing or embroidering, pine trees with sap running into small clay pots attached to their trunks.

The familiar smell of it all, the pine trees, the resin, the rock-rose, the heather, the heath.

The tiny cafés that pop up everywhere, on any bend in the road, any alleyway or street corner—two or three chairs that don't match, a narrow table and a chequered tablecloth, and hey presto.

Coffee drunk from small cups, dark and strong like ours, but with dregs at the bottom. Refreshing light wines like our vinho verde, and ouzo, of course.

People lingering on esplanades, savouring the post-lunch moment, the village taverns and cafés, which were practically only populated by men, for the women disappeared into the backs of houses, a clear division of duties, spaces, habits, rights and time. You could sense both change and resistance to change; that the cities were very different to these lost villages we came across, rural and off the map.

"Kafenio," we heard people say, in a language that sounded like birdsong, full of vowels. We spelt it out on signs, pleased with ourselves whenever we managed to decipher a word.

I could only stand the shouts of the tour guides in small doses, the tourist hordes, the famous sites. I preferred places that had neither name nor history; getting lost in the backstreets, catching glimpses of people's day-to-day lives, buying old postcards at news stands and in traditional Athens shops. Or sitting in a café and looking at the sea.

We almost always ate outside, because the nights were warm and filled with the scent of orange blossom.

I recalled the night we went up Mount Lycabettus together to see the lights of Athens spread out below.

I looked back at the photos we took of the Acropolis, or in Delphi, Crete, Corinth, the islands of Corfu, Myknos, Kos, Santorini, Ithaca—Ithaca, which we also visited, in the Ionian Sea, and which is also only linked to Ulysses in legend.

"The Atlantic. An ocean, not a sea," you said, referring to the paintings in the *Navigations* series.

On a sheet of paper in a frame, you'd written:

Letter to my father:

A single phrase repeated endlessly:

You were not there you were not there you were not there you were not there whenever I needed you you were not there you were not there you were not there you were not there whenever I needed you you were not there you were not there you were not there whenever I needed you you were not there you were not there whenever I needed you you were no

—the whole sheet of paper covered in your handwriting, with no margins or breaks, stopping mid-sentence, mid-word, having run out of space, but as if you might continue onto the next page, and the page after that, indefinitely. And the last visible word was "no."

(A country from which men departed. Had done for centuries. Where, at least until recently, children were left with their mothers while the men continued to distance themselves, retreating into the television or barricading themselves behind newspapers.

You never knew, would never know, Cecilia, that one night, after you'd left, I too wrote a Letter to my Father. Different than yours, but maybe not as different as all that.)

And there was the series *Stories from Near and Far:*

"Mermaids," "Triton Blowing into his Shell," "Dona Marinha."

And horses running through a field. In the *Stockholm Notebooks* you retold the old legend:
"On Mount Tagro, where Lisbon sits, mares are impregnated by the breeze alone."

Pieces of paper spill out a half-open suitcase on the floor. *Almost a Novel,* they say, recalling, projecting, or inventing a narrative, which was then repeated and multiplied in film and video images, of a boat departing, for example, to the sound of the river lapping against the banks—Lisbon becoming further and further away until it's gone—

and then suddenly, when we move a little further on, we're hit by the smell of sea air, as if a window has opened up inside us,

and on a giant screen, occupying an entire wall, sea images flash up hypnotically, obsessively, while the light gradually changes as if the day were unfolding;

deconstructed fado music provides the soundtrack; no word is properly audible, but the subliminal melody is unmistakeable, rising and falling and sometimes disappearing, like a wave on the sand.

From the *Stockholm Notebooks*:
And there's fado, the music of Lisbon . . .
It was first sung at least a hundred and fifty years ago, among the lowest social orders, in backstreets and houses of ill repute, where the divas were working girls and the crooners were sailors and thugs.
Fado isn't melancholic, it's proud. There's defiance in the gestures, a shake of the head, chin held high, chest thrust forward, nothing to hide, acknowledging and accepting who you are, anyone who doesn't want to hear me sing can leave, anyone who's not enjoying the night can leave.
"This is the way I am," goes one of the songs. "God forgive me, if it's a crime or sin. But this is the way I am."

This is the way we are. Mixed and interbred, our blood and our soil, a product of myriad peoples, myriad races. This is the way we are, this is our identity. We may be small, our lives may not amount to much, but life itself is small and millions of small lives make the world go round.

We are common and banal, lovers and loveless, betraying each other, falling into misfortune, settling scores and taking revenge. And laughing too, ridiculing, provoking, denouncing. A voice thrown out there, making itself heard, making itself count. Let it be known: I, Zé Nobody, said this and that, sang the other, pronounced and denounced the rest. Fado speaks of fighting for survival, of injustice, the haves and have nots. It's a song of grief, but also of resistance and revolt.

Women sing fado with their heads held high, men with their hands in their pockets, with the defiant air of the thug. Defiant in the face of life. Life bites us like a rabid dog, but here we are, still standing. And singing and telling, a chronicle of everyday life, there's no time for romanticising, people aren't saints, they make the most of what cunning they've got, because you can get away with anything if you're a shark, but the small fry are always done for in the end.

Sometimes the rhythm is rushed—"corrido"—and can abruptly switch from singing to reciting. O Marceneiro, for example, was always moving back and forth between song and spoken word, he who had no singing voice to speak of, but sang like few others nevertheless. His name was Alfredo Duarte but he was known as O Marceneiro, "The Joiner," for that was his trade, besides singing. And to accompany his song "A Casa da Mariquinhas," he made a model house out of wood, which is a work of modern art, an installation, though he doesn't know it.

Before the great poets turned their hand to fado, the lyrics were written by unknown neighborhood bards who almost no one had heard of. But even when they were at their most pedestrian, all of a sudden one line would leap out and elevate the whole.

Fado is sparing with words, holding them back or speaking them through gritted teeth. Less is more, half-a-dozen lines, generally in quatrains of seven syllables. A syncopated song, with standard phrasing either ignored or revised. The end of a line might skip onto the next one, or interrupt it halfway through, forcing listeners to try and keep track of what was said or miss out on the meaning. Thus verbal language is deconstructed care of musical language, with the two seemingly at odds. Fado anticipates or delays the next phrase, introduces gaps where none are expected, rushes over a run of words to place surprising emphasis elsewhere, all in a manner that might appear accidental. But the lyrical and melodic planes come together in the end. And everything ends up having been said just so.

The classical guitar and Portuguese guitar are complicit, of course, playing a game of cat and mouse with the voice, supporting and echoing it. In the meantime other instruments have come in, the song is transformed while at the same time remaining the same, like all living things.

But people no longer dance, fado has become too independent a musical form for that. It stopped being danced to a long time ago, but at the beginning that's largely what it was for, to rub navels, as sensual and infamous as tango.

The sensuality stayed. Fado is sung with the body.

On a replica of the façade of the house where Fernando Pessoa was born, you've written excerpts from his *Maritime Ode*, which a recorded voice recites.

Then silence falls abruptly, and from out of the silence a bell chimes, each note falling like a drop of water upon a stagnant Lisbon afternoon, and a voice tells us a secret from Pessoa, the city's poet:

"*The bell in my village, Gaspar Simões, is the Church of the Martyrs bell, here in Chiado. I was born in the village of Largo de São Carlos.*"

Meanwhile, there's an intentionally kitsch T-shirt, the sort sold on any Lisbon street, thrown on the floor, crumpled, dirty with salt and boat oil, upon which the slogan *Lisbon is for lovers* can be read, and projected all around the room, at eye level, are slides of anonymous lovers, their faces slightly hidden, just like millions of other people going about the city.

And there are the pictures from the series *The Animal Yard*, a sort of court zoo that housed exotic animals, but where kings, counts, dukes and marquises are also on display, 'rare birds,' out of the ordinary, in strange, comical caricatures. The same mixture of humour and otherness appears again in the series *Patron Saints Dancing* and *The Puppets' Party*.

The eighteenth-century Lisbon notion of life as theatre over-flowed into other paintings too:
   The Royal Factory of Ivory Combs Cardboard Boxes and Varnish,
   The Royal Factory of Silk and Hats,
   in which grotesque figures have leisure and luxury items rain down upon them; playing cards, flowery buttons, braids, scarves, hats and silk ribbons.

From the *Lisbon Notebooks*:

   A sense of Africa can sneak up on you in Lisbon. Palm trees sweeping the sky with their enormous leaves. They acclimatized well, and now they belong here too. It's the first thing you notice when you come out of the airport. Like a warning: we may be in Europe, but our heart is African.
   [. . .]
   The very low houses in Belém and other old areas. The very narrow buildings with verandas, painted in strong colours, yellow,

ochre, green, dark red, blue, pale pink or hot pink, it doesn't matter
whether individual colors go together if you use them at once, like
in the African fabrics women wrap around their bodies, known as
capulanas in Mozambique.

There were films and slides of thousands of faces at rush hour,
crowds getting on and off boats at Terreiro do Paço, faces of all
colours and voices speaking a mixture of languages on the streets
of Mouraria, and in the middle of all this was an installation

The Earth's Journey I:
A wide entrance full of light and colour, like in an old
children's story: images of exotic animals and spices—cinnamon,
pepper, cloves—and the caption:
The faraway becomes near, the exotic is exotic no more, new
flora and fauna grow familiar, spices become part of our lives,
but as the visitors advance, they find themselves entering a
labyrinth, which gets increasingly dark, with phrases flashing
up on the walls:
But what do we know about people?
Nothing.
We are strangers, we never cross the divide between us and those
different to us, we demonize or idealize them,
and suddenly the corridor becomes so narrow that only one
visitor will fit at a time, and all around, on the floor, ceiling and
walls, violent images appear, of torture and death, of bodies and
faces blown up by bombs and gunfire,
Images and sounds so violent they become unbearable and
visitors, feeling they've entered a nightmare, are desperate to
find a way out. But they end up bumping into a mirror that's
as dark as a bottomless well, as just when they expect to come
face-to-face with some horror, suddenly the mirror it lights up
and their own face is reflected back, with the caption:
THE OTHER IS YOU.

A giant screen with images of astronauts coming out of capsules in space stations. The title

The Earth's Journey II

appears projected against a backdrop of blue, the blue of the sea and sky, the color of the *Enigma*.

Space travel as a continuation of the great sea voyages of the fifteenth century, an astonishing scientific and technological achievement, expanding horizons and knowledge, but also (if I've understood your intention) still fleeing into the future instead of correcting the mistakes of our past.

Hence the caption, projected in giant letters, one letter at a time, endlessly:

Earth is the Priority. Earth is the Priority.

From the *Lisbon Notebooks*:

Who are we, launching ourselves into space, where we may or may not find more intelligent life?

What have we achieved with our intelligence, wealth, and technology on the planet we already inhabit?

Our species wasn't destined to survive and evolve, any more than butterflies and cockroaches were, for example. It just accidentally stumbled upon a way out and was transformed. But even after millions of years, we're still only just beginning, and our evolution so far hasn't been very impressive.

The last piece is the installation *Nostos,*: planet Earth, precariously balanced on Ulysses' raft.

The Earth seems to be as light as a soap bubble. Will it find a harbour? Will it find anywhere to make a home for its billions of drifting inhabitants?

The raft is fragile and every so often it goes under, submerged by giant waves, then floats to the surface again looking increasingly unsteady. Bobbing up and down on the raft, the Earth very slowly changes colour, from blue to black to red to the colour of fire, as if aflame, then it goes white, seemingly reduced to ashes, until a weak green colour appears, shining feebly. Perhaps suggesting that, in spite of everything, there is hope. (Your optimism, Cecília, your irrepressible optimism.)

Nevertheless, the green is faint, its glow very slight. And the word *Nostos* ("going home" in Greek) is followed not by a full-stop but by an uneasy comma, a brief pause for breath. As if wishing to leave us with a sense of alarm. Because probably, in the best case scenario, we'll continue our struggle to remain on the surface of the earth while giant waves crash over us. Going home, earth as an inhabitable place for starving, homeless, displaced human beings, the utopia that will perhaps—but for how long?—keep us afloat.

The phone rang at two or three in the morning, on one of the occasions when I worked through the night. I heard Sara's voice.

She'd been burning the midnight oil too, she said, working on a difficult trial that was thankfully coming to a close. The judgement was due any day, after which she was planning to go on holiday to the northeast coast of Brazil.

"Get away for a while. I need a warm beach and some sun."

I had been working day and night, the opening of the exhibition had never been put back, even though it often seemed it would be literally impossible to get everything finished on time.

They were feverish weeks, working with a team of technicians and other workers to transform the space and bring the project into being. A city that was both imaginary and real. Looking out at the world.

I immersed myself in the work, not realising how tired I was or where the time went.

Then one day the exhibition was finally ready and I could walk through it as the first, and until then the only visitor. It came to life around me, gained meaning, embraced me with all its power, vibration and light. Lisbon was there, as we'd loved it, holding itself back and then opening itself up to the gaze of visitors like a succession of mirrors. Mirrors of water.

I walked through the *City of Ulysses* from one end to the other, as if you were there too—and you came with me, Cecília, or rather I took you with me, all the way to the other side. At the furthest point, where the exhibition ended, you'd be born.

You'd enter the world of art, and you'd have a place and a name there forevermore: Cecília Branco.

But it was also there, where the exhibition came to an end, that I realized I'd have to leave you.

You'd moved beyond me and my existence. Your name would have a life of its own. Whatever your work was destined for, it was no one's concern but yours. You were by yourself, on the threshold of a brave new world, and I accepted the inevitability of losing you. Like Orpheus, who left Eurydice in the shadows and walked on without her into the light.

What was left of you was your artistic output. Your corpus. But you were dead. And your ashes had been scattered and mixed into the Lisbon earth.

I walked around the Gulbenkian gardens for a while, among the trees, imagining the excitement, the party, the glitz of the exhibition opening, which I wasn't going to attend.

My work was done, and it was time for me to exit the scene. I'd leave you with your family, which you'd built and loved, who you deserved and who deserved you; I'd leave you with your audience, with the world you'd worked for that would now come to admire you.

I phoned Sara.

"I've finished," I said.

"When's the opening?"

"Tonight. But I'm not staying for it, it belongs in the past now. I've done what I had to do. Are you still thinking of a beach in northeast Brazil?"

"I'm there now. I got here yesterday," she said.

"I'll come and meet you. What's the address of the hotel?"

She gave it to me.

"I'll be waiting for you," she said. And then she added: "I've always been waiting for you. All my life."

"See you soon. I love you," I replied. Because now I could say everything to her.

The plane took off, rising higher and higher. On the other side of the Atlantic, a woman was waiting for me. And I would cross the sea because my love for her was as great as the sea, the love she'd been waiting a lifetime to find.

I imagined myself going up in the hotel lift, stepping into the room, taking her in my arms and falling onto the bed with her, and Molly Bloom's final monologue came to mind. But I preferred Homer's version; after all, he was the finest of storytellers. I rejected Joyce and his disillusionment, that torrent of words, because life didn't have to be the way he saw it. In fact, it hardly needed words at all. The most beautiful of stories, Ulysses' story, could be told with very few:

A man overcame all the obstacles in his path and finally returned to the woman he loved, who had waited for him her whole life.

For millennia, men and women had waited for this story to happen to them. And from time to time, perhaps not so often, and perhaps only for those happy few touched by fortune and the luck of the Gods, this improbable tale of a homecoming came to life, came true.

TEOLINDA GERSÃO was born in Coimbra (Portugal) and has lived in Germany, São Paulo, and Mozambique. She is the author of sixteen books, novels, and short story collections, translated into twelve languages. In 2015 she won the Fernando Namora Prize in Portugal.

JETHRO SOUTAR is a translator of Portuguese and Spanish. His translation of *By Night The Mountain Burns* by Juan Tomás Ávila Laurel was shortlisted for the 2015 Independent Foreign Fiction Prize.

ANNIE MCDERMOTT translates fiction and poetry from Spanish and Portuguese, and her work has appeared in publications such as *Granta*, *World Literature Today*, *Asymptote*, *The Missing Slate*, and *Two Lines*. She has previously lived in Mexico City and São Paulo, Brazil, and is now based in London.

MICHAL AJVAZ, *The Golden Age.*
The Other City.
PIERRE ALBERT-BIROT, *Grabinoulor.*
YUZ ALESHKOVSKY, *Kangaroo.*
FELIPE ALFAU, *Chromos.*
Locos.
JOE AMATO, *Samuel Taylor's Last Night.*
IVAN ÂNGELO, *The Celebration.*
The Tower of Glass.
ANTÓNIO LOBO ANTUNES, *Knowledge of Hell.*
The Splendor of Portugal.
ALAIN ARIAS-MISSON, *Theatre of Incest.*
JOHN ASHBERY & JAMES SCHUYLER, *A Nest of Ninnies.*
ROBERT ASHLEY, *Perfect Lives.*
GABRIELA AVIGUR-ROTEM, *Heatwave and Crazy Birds.*
DJUNA BARNES, *Ladies Almanack.*
Ryder.
JOHN BARTH, *Letters.*
Sabbatical.
DONALD BARTHELME, *The King.*
Paradise.
SVETISLAV BASARA, *Chinese Letter.*
MIQUEL BAUÇÀ, *The Siege in the Room.*
RENÉ BELLETTO, *Dying.*
MAREK BIENCZYK, *Transparency.*
ANDREI BITOV, *Pushkin House.*
ANDREJ BLATNIK, *You Do Understand.*
Law of Desire.
LOUIS PAUL BOON, *Chapel Road.*
My Little War.
Summer in Termuren.
ROGER BOYLAN, *Killoyle.*
IGNÁCIO DE LOYOLA BRANDÃO, *Anonymous Celebrity.*
Zero.
BONNIE BREMSER, *Troia: Mexican Memoirs.*
CHRISTINE BROOKE-ROSE, *Amalgamemnon.*
BRIGID BROPHY, *In Transit.*
The Prancing Novelist.

GERALD L. BRUNS, *Modern Poetry and the Idea of Language.*
GABRIELLE BURTON, *Heartbreak Hotel.*
MICHEL BUTOR, *Degrees.*
Mobile.
G. CABRERA INFANTE, *Infante's Inferno.*
Three Trapped Tigers.
JULIETA CAMPOS, *The Fear of Losing Eurydice.*
ANNE CARSON, *Eros the Bittersweet.*
ORLY CASTEL-BLOOM, *Dolly City.*
LOUIS-FERDINAND CÉLINE, *North.*
Conversations with Professor Y.
London Bridge.
MARIE CHAIX, *The Laurels of Lake Constance.*
HUGO CHARTERIS, *The Tide Is Right.*
ERIC CHEVILLARD, *Demolishing Nisard.*
The Author and Me.
MARC CHOLODENKO, *Mordechai Schamz.*
JOSHUA COHEN, *Witz.*
EMILY HOLMES COLEMAN, *The Shutter of Snow.*
ERIC CHEVILLARD, *The Author and Me.*
ROBERT COOVER, *A Night at the Movies.*
STANLEY CRAWFORD, *Log of the S.S. The Mrs Unguentine.*
Some Instructions to My Wife.
RENÉ CREVEL, *Putting My Foot in It.*
RALPH CUSACK, *Cadenza.*
NICHOLAS DELBANCO, *Sherbrookes.*
The Count of Concord.
NIGEL DENNIS, *Cards of Identity.*
PETER DIMOCK, *A Short Rhetoric for Leaving the Family.*
ARIEL DORFMAN, *Konfidenz.*
COLEMAN DOWELL, *Island People.*
Too Much Flesh and Jabez.
ARKADII DRAGOMOSHCHENKO, *Dust.*
RIKKI DUCORNET, *Phosphor in Dreamland.*
The Complete Butcher's Tales.

RIKKI DUCORNET (cont.), *The Jade Cabinet.*
The Fountains of Neptune.
WILLIAM EASTLAKE, *The Bamboo Bed.*
Castle Keep.
Lyric of the Circle Heart.
JEAN ECHENOZ, *Chopin's Move.*
STANLEY ELKIN, *A Bad Man.*
Criers and Kibitzers, Kibitzers and Criers.
The Dick Gibson Show.
The Franchiser.
The Living End.
Mrs. Ted Bliss.
FRANÇOIS EMMANUEL, *Invitation to a Voyage.*
PAUL EMOND, *The Dance of a Sham.*
SALVADOR ESPRIU, *Ariadne in the Grotesque Labyrinth.*
LESLIE A. FIEDLER, *Love and Death in the American Novel.*
JUAN FILLOY, *Op Oloop.*
ANDY FITCH, *Pop Poetics.*
GUSTAVE FLAUBERT, *Bouvard and Pécuchet.*
KASS FLEISHER, *Talking out of School.*
JON FOSSE, *Aliss at the Fire.*
Melancholy.
FORD MADOX FORD, *The March of Literature.*
MAX FRISCH, *I'm Not Stiller.*
Man in the Holocene.
CARLOS FUENTES, *Christopher Unborn.*
Distant Relations.
Terra Nostra.
Where the Air Is Clear.
TAKEHIKO FUKUNAGA, *Flowers of Grass.*
WILLIAM GADDIS, JR., *The Recognitions.*
JANICE GALLOWAY, *Foreign Parts.*
The Trick Is to Keep Breathing.
WILLIAM H. GASS, *Life Sentences.*
The Tunnel.
The World Within the Word.
Willie Masters' Lonesome Wife.
GÉRARD GAVARRY, *Hoppla! 1 2 3.*

ETIENNE GILSON, *The Arts of the Beautiful.*
Forms and Substances in the Arts.
C. S. GISCOMBE, *Giscome Road.*
Here.
DOUGLAS GLOVER, *Bad News of the Heart.*
WITOLD GOMBROWICZ, *A Kind of Testament.*
PAULO EMÍLIO SALES GOMES, *P's Three Women.*
GEORGI GOSPODINOV, *Natural Novel.*
JUAN GOYTISOLO, *Count Julian.*
Juan the Landless.
Makbara.
Marks of Identity.
HENRY GREEN, *Blindness.*
Concluding.
Doting.
Nothing.
JACK GREEN, *Fire the Bastards!*
JIŘÍ GRUŠA, *The Questionnaire.*
MELA HARTWIG, *Am I a Redundant Human Being?*
JOHN HAWKES, *The Passion Artist.*
Whistlejacket.
ELIZABETH HEIGHWAY, ED., *Contemporary Georgian Fiction.*
AIDAN HIGGINS, *Balcony of Europe.*
Blind Man's Bluff.
Bornholm Night-Ferry.
Langrishe, Go Down.
Scenes from a Receding Past.
KEIZO HINO, *Isle of Dreams.*
KAZUSHI HOSAKA, *Plainsong.*
ALDOUS HUXLEY, *Antic Hay.*
Point Counter Point.
Those Barren Leaves.
Time Must Have a Stop.
NAOYUKI II, *The Shadow of a Blue Cat.*
DRAGO JANČAR, *The Tree with No Name.*
MIKHEIL JAVAKHISHVILI, *Kvachi.*
GERT JONKE, *The Distant Sound.*
Homage to Czerny.
The System of Vienna.

JACQUES JOUET, *Mountain R.*
Savage.
Upstaged.

MIEKO KANAI, *The Word Book.*

YORAM KANIUK, *Life on Sandpaper.*

ZURAB KARUMIDZE, *Dagny.*

JOHN KELLY, *From Out of the City.*

HUGH KENNER, *Flaubert, Joyce and Beckett: The Stoic Comedians.*
Joyce's Voices.

DANILO KIŠ, *The Attic.*
The Lute and the Scars.
Psalm 44.
A Tomb for Boris Davidovich.

ANITA KONKKA, *A Fool's Paradise.*

GEORGE KONRÁD, *The City Builder.*

TADEUSZ KONWICKI, *A Minor Apocalypse.*
The Polish Complex.

ANNA KORDZAIA-SAMADASHVILI, *Me, Margarita.*

MENIS KOUMANDAREAS, *Koula.*

ELAINE KRAF, *The Princess of 72nd Street.*

JIM KRUSOE, *Iceland.*

AYSE KULIN, *Farewell: A Mansion in Occupied Istanbul.*

EMILIO LASCANO TEGUI, *On Elegance While Sleeping.*

ERIC LAURRENT, *Do Not Touch.*

VIOLETTE LEDUC, *La Bâtarde.*

EDOUARD LEVÉ, *Autoportrait.*
Newspaper.
Suicide.
Works.

MARIO LEVI, *Istanbul Was a Fairy Tale.*

DEBORAH LEVY, *Billy and Girl.*

JOSÉ LEZAMA LIMA, *Paradiso.*

ROSA LIKSOM, *Dark Paradise.*

OSMAN LINS, *Avalovara.*
The Queen of the Prisons of Greece.

FLORIAN LIPUŠ, *The Errors of Young Tjaž.*

GORDON LISH, *Peru.*

ALF MACLOCHLAINN, *Out of Focus.*
Past Habitual.

The Corpus in the Library.

RON LOEWINSOHN, *Magnetic Field(s).*

YURI LOTMAN, *Non-Memoirs.*

D. KEITH MANO, *Take Five.*

MINA LOY, *Stories and Essays of Mina Loy.*

MICHELINE AHARONIAN MARCOM, *A Brief History of Yes.*
The Mirror in the Well.

BEN MARCUS, *The Age of Wire and String.*

WALLACE MARKFIELD, *Teitlebaum's Window.*

DAVID MARKSON, *Reader's Block.*
Wittgenstein's Mistress.

CAROLE MASO, *AVA.*

HISAKI MATSUURA, *Triangle.*

LADISLAV MATEJKA & KRYSTYNA POMORSKA, EDS., *Readings in Russian Poetics: Formalist & Structuralist Views.*

HARRY MATHEWS, *Cigarettes.*
The Conversions.
The Human Country.
The Journalist.
My Life in CIA.
Singular Pleasures.
The Sinking of the Odradek.
Stadium.
Tlooth.

HISAKI MATSUURA, *Triangle.*

DONAL MCLAUGHLIN, *beheading the virgin mary, and other stories.*

JOSEPH MCELROY, *Night Soul and Other Stories.*

ABDELWAHAB MEDDEB, *Talismano.*

GERHARD MEIER, *Isle of the Dead.*

HERMAN MELVILLE, *The Confidence-Man.*

AMANDA MICHALOPOULOU, *I'd Like.*

STEVEN MILLHAUSER, *The Barnum Museum.*
In the Penny Arcade.

RALPH J. MILLS, JR., *Essays on Poetry.*

MOMUS, *The Book of Jokes.*

CHRISTINE MONTALBETTI, *The Origin of Man.*
Western.

NICHOLAS MOSLEY, *Accident.*
Assassins.
Catastrophe Practice.
A Garden of Trees.
Hopeful Monsters.
Imago Bird.
Inventing God.
Look at the Dark.
Metamorphosis.
Natalie Natalia.
Serpent.

WARREN MOTTE, *Fables of the Novel: French Fiction since 1990.*
Fiction Now: The French Novel in the 21st Century.
Mirror Gazing.
Oulipo: A Primer of Potential Literature.

GERALD MURNANE, *Barley Patch.*
Inland.

YVES NAVARRE, *Our Share of Time.*
Sweet Tooth.

DOROTHY NELSON, *In Night's City.*
Tar and Feathers.

ESHKOL NEVO, *Homesick.*

WILFRIDO D. NOLLEDO, *But for the Lovers.*

BORIS A. NOVAK, *The Master of Insomnia.*

FLANN O'BRIEN, *At Swim-Two-Birds.*
The Best of Myles.
The Dalkey Archive.
The Hard Life.
The Poor Mouth.
The Third Policeman.

CLAUDE OLLIER, *The Mise-en-Scène.*
Wert and the Life Without End.

PATRIK OUŘEDNÍK, *Europeana.*
The Opportune Moment, 1855.

BORIS PAHOR, *Necropolis.*

FERNANDO DEL PASO, *News from the Empire.*
Palinuro of Mexico.

ROBERT PINGET, *The Inquisitory.*
Mahu or The Material.
Trio.

MANUEL PUIG, *Betrayed by Rita Hayworth.*

The Buenos Aires Affair.
Heartbreak Tango.

RAYMOND QUENEAU, *The Last Days.*
Odile.
Pierrot Mon Ami.
Saint Glinglin.

ANN QUIN, *Berg.*
Passages.
Three.
Tripticks.

ISHMAEL REED, *The Free-Lance Pallbearers.*
The Last Days of Louisiana Red.
Ishmael Reed: The Plays.
Juice!
The Terrible Threes.
The Terrible Twos.
Yellow Back Radio Broke-Down.

JASIA REICHARDT, *15 Journeys Warsaw to London.*

JOÃO UBALDO RIBEIRO, *House of the Fortunate Buddhas.*

JEAN RICARDOU, *Place Names.*

RAINER MARIA RILKE,
The Notebooks of Malte Laurids Brigge.

JULIÁN RÍOS, *The House of Ulysses.*
Larva: A Midsummer Night's Babel.
Poundemonium.

ALAIN ROBBE-GRILLET, *Project for a Revolution in New York.*
A Sentimental Novel.

AUGUSTO ROA BASTOS, *I the Supreme.*

DANIËL ROBBERECHTS, *Arriving in Avignon.*

JEAN ROLIN, *The Explosion of the Radiator Hose.*

OLIVIER ROLIN, *Hotel Crystal.*

ALIX CLEO ROUBAUD, *Alix's Journal.*

JACQUES ROUBAUD, *The Form of a City Changes Faster, Alas, Than the Human Heart.*
The Great Fire of London.
Hortense in Exile.
Hortense Is Abducted.
Mathematics: The Plurality of Worlds of Lewis.
Some Thing Black.

RAYMOND ROUSSEL, *Impressions of Africa.*

VEDRANA RUDAN, *Night.*

PABLO M. RUIZ, *Four Cold Chapters on the Possibility of Literature.*

GERMAN SADULAEV, *The Maya Pill.*

TOMAŽ ŠALAMUN, *Soy Realidad.*

LYDIE SALVAYRE, *The Company of Ghosts.*
The Lecture.
The Power of Flies.

LUIS RAFAEL SÁNCHEZ, *Macho Camacho's Beat.*

SEVERO SARDUY, *Cobra & Maitreya.*

NATHALIE SARRAUTE, *Do You Hear Them?*
Martereau.
The Planetarium.

STIG SÆTERBAKKEN, *Siamese.*
Self-Control.
Through the Night.

ARNO SCHMIDT, *Collected Novellas.*
Collected Stories.
Nobodaddy's Children.
Two Novels.

ASAF SCHURR, *Motti.*

GAIL SCOTT, *My Paris.*

DAMION SEARLS, *What We Were Doing and Where We Were Going.*

JUNE AKERS SEESE,
Is This What Other Women Feel Too?

BERNARD SHARE, *Inish.*
Transit.

VIKTOR SHKLOVSKY, *Bowstring.*
Literature and Cinematography.
Theory of Prose.
Third Factory.
Zoo, or Letters Not about Love.

PIERRE SINIAC, *The Collaborators.*

KJERSTI A. SKOMSVOLD,
The Faster I Walk, the Smaller I Am.

JOSEF ŠKVORECKÝ, *The Engineer of Human Souls.*

GILBERT SORRENTINO, *Aberration of Starlight.*
Blue Pastoral.
Crystal Vision.

Imaginative Qualities of Actual Things.
Mulligan Stew. Red the Fiend.
Steelwork.
Under the Shadow.

MARKO SOSIČ, *Ballerina, Ballerina.*

ANDRZEJ STASIUK, *Dukla.*
Fado.

GERTRUDE STEIN, *The Making of Americans.*
A Novel of Thank You.

LARS SVENDSEN, *A Philosophy of Evil.*

PIOTR SZEWC, *Annihilation.*

GONÇALO M. TAVARES, *A Man: Klaus Klump.*
Jerusalem.
Learning to Pray in the Age of Technique.

LUCIAN DAN TEODOROVICI,
Our Circus Presents…

NIKANOR TERATOLOGEN, *Assisted Living.*

STEFAN THEMERSON, *Hobson's Island.*
The Mystery of the Sardine.
Tom Harris.

TAEKO TOMIOKA, *Building Waves.*

JOHN TOOMEY, *Sleepwalker.*

DUMITRU TSEPENEAG, *Hotel Europa.*
The Necessary Marriage.
Pigeon Post.
Vain Art of the Fugue.

ESTHER TUSQUETS, *Stranded.*

DUBRAVKA UGRESIC, *Lend Me Your Character.*
Thank You for Not Reading.

TOR ULVEN, *Replacement.*

MATI UNT, *Brecht at Night.*
Diary of a Blood Donor.
Things in the Night.

ÁLVARO URIBE & OLIVIA SEARS, EDS.,
Best of Contemporary Mexican Fiction.

ELOY URROZ, *Friction.*
The Obstacles.

LUISA VALENZUELA, *Dark Desires and the Others.*
He Who Searches.

PAUL VERHAEGHEN, *Omega Minor.*

BORIS VIAN, *Heartsnatcher.*

LLORENÇ VILLALONGA, *The Dolls'
Room.*

TOOMAS VINT, *An Unending Landscape.*

ORNELA VORPSI, *The Country Where No
One Ever Dies.*

AUSTRYN WAINHOUSE, *Hedyphagetica.*

CURTIS WHITE, *America's Magic
Mountain.*
The Idea of Home.
Memories of My Father Watching TV.
Requiem.

DIANE WILLIAMS,
Excitability: Selected Stories.
Romancer Erector.

DOUGLAS WOOLF, *Wall to Wall.*
Ya! & John-Juan.

JAY WRIGHT, *Polynomials and Pollen.*
The Presentable Art of Reading Absence.

PHILIP WYLIE, *Generation of Vipers.*

MARGUERITE YOUNG, *Angel in the
Forest.*
Miss MacIntosh, My Darling.

REYOUNG, *Unbabbling.*

VLADO ŽABOT, *The Succubus.*

ZORAN ŽIVKOVIĆ , *Hidden Camera.*

LOUIS ZUKOFSKY, *Collected Fiction.*

VITOMIL ZUPAN, *Minuet for Guitar.*

SCOTT ZWIREN, *God Head.*

AND MORE . . .